THE STAR OF GNOSIA

Damian Murphy is the author of *The Academy Outside of Ingolstadt, Seduction of the Golden Pheasant, The Exaltation of the Minotaur*, and *Daughters of Apostasy*, among other collections and novellas. His work has been published on the Mount Abraxas, Les Éditions de L'Oubli, and L'Homme Récent imprints of Ex Occidente Press, in Bucharest, and by Zagava Books, in Dusseldorf. He was born and lives in Seattle, Washington.

SNUGGLY BOOKS

DAMIAN MURPHY

THE STAR OF GNOSIA

THIS IS A SNUGGLY BOOK

ISBN: 978-1-943813-72-8

The Imperishable Sacraments was first published by Ex Occidente Press/L'Homme Recent, 2015. "The Apostatical Ascetic" was first published under the pseudonym Alexander Search in *Dreams of Ourselves: An Appreciation of Pessoa*, edited by Adolph Moscow, Ex Occidente Press/L'Homme Recent, 2014. "A Perilous Ordeal" was first published in *A Distillate of Heresy,* Ex Occidente Press/Les Éditions de L'Oubli, 2014. "The Hour of the Minotaur" was first published in *The Gift of the Kosmos Cometh! A Homage to Night and Kosmos*, edited by Geticus Polus and Damian Murphy, Ex Occidente Press/L'Homme Recent, 2016. "The Star of Gnosia" is original to this volume.

For the sibylantic minotaur whose house lies on the border of Beijing and Berlin. And for Mallarmé, the master thief, who sucked the starlight out of night's imperishable splendor and spat it out in salutation to the idiot savants.

Contents

THE STAR OF GNOSIA

The Imperishable Sacraments

"This is the night of which it is written: The night shall be as bright as day."

Vespers

THE AUSPICES of dusk graced the quiet courtyard. Long shadows fell like the beards of ancient prophets over the flaking yellow paint, the dilapidated wooden door frames, the obtrusive iron bars set firmly into place over the windows. Simone slipped through a rusty gate and onto the unwashed tiles, a rolled up paper bag nestled securely under one arm. Her dark red velvet skirt extended nearly all the way to the tops of her high, black shoes. She stepped through a crumbling doorway which lay beneath a veil of shadow to one side, walked down a short concrete stairway adorned with ivy, and followed the bend around to the back of the old tenement building.

The narrow thoroughfare was seldom used. The back windows looked out onto an uninspiring concrete wall coated with grime and moss. Every single one of the tenants who occupied that side of the building kept their back blinds drawn. A paved walkway ran just below the level of the basement windows, terminating before a wooden fence. Pale blue shadows lay supine upon the pavement. Simone traversed the narrow passage as if it was a holy place.

She set the rolled up paper bag down near the end of the walkway. The reverence of her concentrated gaze was nearly concealed by a head of dark brown, chin-length hair. She began to remove the contents of the bag, piece by piece, arranging them with meticulous care upon the concrete surface.

First came a chipped and splintered square of wood roughly the size of a chessboard, which she placed on the ground before her. She ran a finger over the patterns in the grain, warped ever so slightly around a knot near one of the outer edges.

Next came a tall red liqueur glass. The short stem supported an expansive bulb topped with a delicately curved lip. This was placed exactly in the center of the board. She removed also a sealed bottle filled with water which had been collected from the sea at a propitious hour, some of the contents of which were poured into the glass, nearly filling it. From a pocket concealed in her skirt she fished out a silver key and dropped it into the salty brine.

She again reached into the depths of the bag, as if it were the very mouth of mystery, and retrieved a small rectangular piece of white paper, exactly like those found hidden within cheap fortune cookies. One side of the paper bore a message, the letters appearing as if they'd been produced on an antiquated typewriter: "Oh, sweep away, Angel, with Angelic Scorn, the Dogs that come with Curious Eyes to gaze." This she placed on the edge of the wood nearest to herself, as if to indicate a title for the piece.

Next were retrieved two tiny ceramic hands, each meticulously painted and missing several fingers. Some of the fingers had been broken, while others were actually sculpted as if the unfortunate hands had been maliciously deformed. Splinters of glaring white bone protruded from bloody stubs, all painted in exquisite detail. At one time, the hands had been attached to the body of a doll of exceptional design. She'd found it in a box, abandoned along with several other items of little interest, by a lonely stretch of railway under a night of immaculate stars. The doll was dressed in a manner which could only be described as operatic, as if it had been intended to resemble an actor on an ostentatious stage. The lips were pursed dramatically, the eyes stared from their sockets like two burning coals, the eyebrows arched as if to curse the hosts of heaven with the impunity afforded only to the deranged. Simone was captivated by the find, though most of her friends found it positively disturbing.

One fine day, after she had scorned a lover of little importance, her brokenhearted suitor grabbed the doll from its alcove by the door as he made his way out of her apartment. He turned to face Simone and, fixing her with a contemptuous gaze, smacked the beloved relic hard against the wall. The hands went flying deep into the hidden recesses of her apartment. The dejected beau tossed the doll carelessly at its owner's feet and never spoke to her again. His destructive act had resulted in the severance of some of the remaining fingers from the palms. As much as this had infuriated her, she was later compelled to admit that the disfiguration of the doll only enhanced its sinister appearance. She'd kept the broken hands among her prized possessions for a year or so, but now it was time to let them go. She placed them with their palms facing down on the front corners of the board.

Finally, she removed a small, black-bound book, no larger than the span between her wrist and the tips of her fingers. The front cover featured three lines of Arabic script decoratively inscribed in gold. The title of the book could be read in her own language on the third page from the cover: *The Kasîdah of Hâjî Abdû El-Yezdî*. She touched the cherished object first to her brow, then to her heart, and finally she graced it with her lips. After a moment's hesitation, she placed it, cover closed, upright against the red liqueur glass.

A tiny candelabra containing three short white candles was placed on the back of the board, behind the glass and book. The graceful, if humble, glow that suffused the altar as the wicks were lit completed the offering. She left the candle burning as she made her way back up the stairs and out through the gate.

Night had begun to fall. The streets were bathed in dark shades of magnificent blue interspersed with the pale yellow glow of the streetlights. Simone passed below high windows which, like stoic sentries, bore witness to the nightly demise of the sun. She strode past crumbling façades of brick and stone, walking briskly as if pursued by treacherous winds. From a narrow street lined with ancient stones she emerged into a brightly lit square, crossed over the paved expanse, and plunged into an alley on the other side. From there she made her way to an unembellished doorway, accompanied by a multitude of shadows cast by the overhanging lamps, and disappeared at last into the confines of her apartment.

✸

Late morning brought a light breakfast of two hard-boiled eggs washed down with a mouthful of champagne taken from a flask. Simone sat on a public bench in a more or less deserted city square, reading from a petite and weathered volume bound in orange and russet. In the mornings, she read from her holy books, an ever-expanding collection of texts which she had imbued with sacerdotal significance. This morning's sacred text, number thirteen of twenty-two, was a time-worn copy of *Locus Solus* by Raymond Roussel. Written in a crisp, affectionless prose wrought with obsessive detail, the text was little more than a catalog of elaborate and fantastical machines. It seemed to serve no discernable purpose as a literary work. The sufferings, ecstasies, mythologies, and revelations found between its covers were rendered with a scientific precision which, paradoxically, bordered on the erotic. Simone had perused her copy of the book so often that many of the pages had come loose from their bindings.

On the other side of the courtyard stood a modest house of God. Within the portal of the church, in a sizable lunette above two heavy wooden doors, was set a heavenly epiphany in smooth white marble. It was a statue of St. Peter, his bearded head bowed in solemn adoration, with one hand wrapped around a closed book while the other held two crossed keys before his heart. Simone had taken note of the stonework before, admiring the air of reverence imparted by its elaborate design. The icon seemed to implicate a secret well concealed. She'd been meaning to visit the interior of the church for some time, but had thus far managed to distract herself with other haunts. Perhaps she'd stop by later in the evening.

After she had finished her breakfast, she made her way uptown to the local symphony hall. Here she worked six short shifts a week in a slightly claustrophobic ticket booth, selling subscriptions, recommending productions, dispensing will-call tickets, and providing other menial services. Her compensation included two free performances per month, of which she never failed to take advantage. She could often be found playing chess out in the lobby with a co-worker after the ticket booths had closed. The music from the hall could be heard with a moderate degree of clarity from the far side of the heavy doors. Though the impact of the orchestra was significantly greater in the auditorium itself, she half-preferred the muffled echoes that accompanied her scrutiny of the chessboard.

Her afternoon shift passed with a minimum of bother. A middle-aged man, at least twice Simone's age and somewhat of a letch, had tried to engage her in conversation, but had succeeded only in eliciting an icy impassivity. Men occasionally approached her booth with the sole intent of soliciting her affections. She had not the slightest bit of interest. She'd had a handful of suitors over the years, none of whom had managed to sustain her devotions for long. A few nights of amorous adventure would inevitably be followed by an intense urge for prolonged solitude. She simply preferred to be alone. She took care to keep her mysteries well concealed so as not to profane them. She had once been told that there was a void where her heart should be. Her response was that her passion withered in the company of others, that her ardor flamed most brightly when untouched by impure hands.

She sometimes amused herself, when maintaining the booth, by determining precisely what it took to compel the more pernicious among her admirers to go away. She'd quote the dictionary at them with a flatness which did little to conceal her contempt, or she'd respond to their attempts at conversation with a single phrase repeated over and over again. Sometimes she pretended to take notes as if conducting a scientific experiment. The inept coquetry of the older man who now stood on the other side of the glass had begun to irritate her. She was just reaching for the dictionary when he at last gave up and purchased a subscription.

She returned to the church just as the sun was going down. Long blue shadows stretched along the courtyard tiles like a slowly creeping tide, bathing the stones in the soft mysteries of sundown. Simone stood before the wide steps leading up to the entrance, pondering the icon of the saint. The motif of the heavenly keys had always intrigued her. Would that it were possible, she would pilfer them. She imagined herself as Gestas, the unrepentant thief who, along with his companion, Dismas, was crucified along-side Christ on Golgotha. In the fires of her inner vision, she and her companion dared to trespass the outer court of heaven. One key was lost to Gestas under cover of the night, while Dismas made off with the other under the auspices of day.

Her ruminations were disturbed as one of the tall wooden doors swung open. An older man dressed in black cassock and skullcap emerged, peering from place to place about the tranquil courtyard. Thin tufts of white hair protruded from beneath his cap and a pair of spectacles adorned his face. He was animated with a nervous fire not entirely devoid of sublimity. He took note of the quality of attention which Simone had been paying to the statue above the door. He hobbled down the three short steps to the cobblestones below and stood beside her, hands clasped behind his back. He regarded the icon with a studious gaze.

"There are mysteries, conceived within the fires of heaven," he said in a thin voice after a moment of concentrated silence, "which can be known only between one hand and the other."

Simone remained silent, clasping her hands together before her with forefingers extended and raised to her lips. Her feet were turned slightly inward.

"The ancient art of rendering eternal truths in stone has by and large been lost to us," the man continued, with an air of resignation. "Its secrets have been scattered through the ages like funerary ashes. There are artists known to us who possess the necessary skill, and who have received the living flame of the tradition, but the light is dimming."

The shadows continued to spread along the courtyard, reaching like pious hands of prayer toward the protruding balconies on the eastern side of the square. Simone turned toward the man, realized that she had absolutely nothing to say to him, and turned again to regard the icon of the saint.

"The mystery of the keys has long confounded the greatest minds of the church," said the man. "They are the keys to the gates of the Kingdom of Heaven—one key loosens, while the other binds. Do you suppose this mystery is generally understood?"

Simone did not suppose a single thing. The man continued.

"Some maintain that the keys have been lost, scattered to the ends of the earth," he adjusted the spectacles on his face, "while others claim that they serve more . . . esoteric purposes. I once laid eyes upon a document, shown to me by a scholar who is kindly disposed to the church, which claims that only one of them opens the gates of Heaven. The other, it is written, unlocks the gates of the infernal regions. There are others who have linked them to the winter and summer solstices, the Lesser and Greater Mysteries of Eleusis, the two opposing faces of the Greek God Janus; in yet another place it has been speculated that one key was forged in the fires of Heaven and the other in the fires of Hell. There is no end to the suppositions of theologians."

Simone was not inclined to comment on the speculations of the priest, if indeed he was a priest. She simply listened, taking in the rhythm and cadence of his speech.

"In the end, what can we know?" the man lamented. "The Holy One resides always beyond the limits of our understanding. His purity cannot be contained by man. A portion of the soul resides with him in the eternal, while that which remains must ultimately drown in the ocean of his mystery."

The use of the male pronoun bristled against Simone's nerves. 'The Absolute cannot be limited to the figure of your miserable patriarch,' she thought. Nevertheless, she couldn't help but be intrigued by the man's ruminations. She wanted to ask if he had any thoughts concerning the book which the saint held clasped against his body, but her tongue refused to form the necessary words.

The man headed back toward the door. He stopped, turned again to Simone, straightened up his spine and briefly cast his eyes heavenward as if to look for rain. A moment passed. Without a word he re-entered the church and closed the door behind him.

Simone felt awkward following the man into the church. She'd had rather enough of him for the time being. She decided to return another day to explore the interior. Seeking ever greater raptures, she headed out into the awaiting arms of the city as it drowsily prepared for the coming sojourn through the night.

Later, having returned to her apartment, she dined on strawberries and slightly stale bread washed down with the remnants of a bottle of chardonnay which had been keeping dubious company in the icebox. Her modest living space, a single room on the fourth floor of an aged building, was filled with relics and icons unfathomable to those uninitiated into her particular mysteries. A bright green typewriter hung above the front door, a Remington portable, the lower lip of which rested on the edge of the doorframe. The machine had been disfigured in a curious manner. Several months before, Simone had pried five of the forty-six keys from their casings: the letters M, U, T, I, and S. These she cast into the sea on a particularly tumultuous night, an offering of silence for the moon in Her guise as the mother of mystery, of prophecy, of purity.

Above the tall bookshelves hung framed squares of canvas adorned with mathematical formulas in a variety of subtle hues and shades. Simone, being perfectly ambidextrous, had painted them all with her left hand. So fanciful was the style of the characters that they looked like sacred incantations. She'd wished to free them from the limitations of the rational mind by which they'd been imprisoned for so long. She had convinced herself that every formula had its own attendant spirit, which, like the numberless angels found in the grimoires of antiquity, bestowed particular virtues upon those so bold as to evoke them.

A wooden cabinet housing twenty-six square niches hung between two windows. Nineteen of the niches harbored keys, each one different from the rest, each of them hanging from brass hooks. The cabinet had been salvaged from the remains of an old hotel shortly before the building was torn down. Simone had an uncanny knack for finding keys in unexpected places. She'd found them lying about in the street, surreptitiously hiding under benches, or abandoned on the surfaces of sewer grates and utility covers. She only took them if she could convince herself, with some degree of certitude, that the key could not be returned to its rightful owner. A key that had been lost, she thought, possessed peculiar qualities. There were doors, she was quite certain, which lay concealed behind the veil of the visible world, doors which granted access to places without names.

A basket half-filled with strawberries remained after Simone had finished her meal. These she arranged with the skilled hand of an aesthete, placing them around a short white candle in a wooden bowl. From a bookshelf, she selected a volume bound in white, one of a series of undecorated books with hand-painted titles. "Tobold," read the spine, "by Robert Walser." She placed the opened volume, the ghost-white pages having not a scrap of writing on them, on a low table before one of the windows. The bowl of strawberries was placed before the book, the candle flaming gently in the dim light. The flickering shadows traced the forms of phantom letters on the empty pages.

Simone felt a deep obligation to the lost works of her favorite authors. Their absence left a space in her imagination which gave rise to dreams unparalleled in richness and splendor. She hoped to nurture the ghosts of these aborted treasures, to cause them to increase in essence until they forced their way back into the world. She invited them to haunt the city, to reveal themselves in unexpected places, to inspire the hands of poets and artists that their lost virtues might be resurrected. They comprised for her a second order of the holy book; an order concealed, hidden, esoteric. A friend of hers, a bookbinder, had created for her a series of blank white books with which she might give substance to these formless phantoms. Among the many empty volumes which sat upon her shelves could be found de Quincey's lost volumes of the *Suspiria de Profundis*, Bruno Schulz's *The Messiah*, and Rimbaud's *La Chasse spirituelle*, along with several others.

The crown jewel of the collection was the *Inventio Fortunata*, a 14th-century document containing a detailed description of an expedition to the uninhabitable regions of the far north. The document, quoted liberally in a letter written by the cartographer Mercator to the renowned astrologer and spy John Dee, purportedly depicted the pole as a towering magnetic rock, thirty-three miles in circumference, surrounded by a vast stretch of land divided nearly equally by four rivers extending outward to the cardinal directions. To Simone, this place was as real as any terrestrial country. Like Dante's Purgatory or the Celestial Jerusalem of Revelation, it existed in a supersensible geography which the soul alone could comprehend, accessible to the visionary, the mystic, and the poet, if not to the cartographer.

A reproduction of Mercator's celebrated *Septentrionalium Terrarum*, which displayed the influence of the lost report in its depiction of the northern regions, hung framed in magnetized iron above the dilapidated sink which protruded from one wall of the kitchenless apartment. Several other maps throughout the 15th and 16th centuries had been similarly influenced. The fabled mountain at the pole had occupied a place of pure mystery in the imaginations of so many that Simone could not help but revere it as a god. She had adopted it as her Kiblah, a place by which to orient herself in regions which could not be measured by mortal hands.

The next morning, after perusing the holy texts of Novalis and de Nerval (numbers eighteen and eleven on her list, respectively), Simone made her way back to the thoroughfare behind the crumbling apartment building to check on the altar which she'd left there. She liked to watch her offerings disperse and scatter over time. Perishables would decay in surprising and horrific ways; birds and other animals would topple the elaborate displays or make off with some of the smaller items; the elements would leave their mark, destroying books and other paper items and filling cups and glasses with rainwater. The slow and unpredictable process of transformation was for her a kind of augury, a mirror of the city and of herself in which she might trace the unseen boundaries of a hidden order.

For the most part, the elements upon the altar had remained exactly where she'd placed them. The hands had not been pilfered, the tall red liqueur glass had not been overturned, though her typewritten title was nowhere to be found, and of course the candles had burned themselves down. A closer inspection, on the other hand, revealed several changes of a type which she had not expected. Some of the objects had been modified, some swapped with other items altogether. Somebody must have discovered her work and rearranged it according to their own design.

The silver key had been taken from the glass of seawater, while the water itself would seem to have been swapped with sweet white wine (or so she judged from the scent). A new key, cast in shining copper, had been placed between the two severed hands, which had been turned to face palm-up.

More startling still was the fact that the book which she had left there had been exchanged for another. The new book was roughly the same size as was the previous one. The cover was of a similar material, though the leather was of a creamy white hue rather than black. A single star appeared embossed upon the front, so subtly that it was difficult to notice at first glance. The book was scuffed along the edges and the pages worn and yellowed. It looked as if it was several decades old.

Simone was intrigued, to say the least. Never before had she encountered such an elaborate response to her handiwork. She studied the arrangement for a time, the constituents of which were no longer entirely her own. The essential nature of the thing had changed in a manner which could not quite be measured. The flavor of the work had been subtly elevated. It had about it an air of sublimity which she had never quite been able to achieve in her own work, as if the hand which had adjusted the design was of a finer nature than hers. After a moment's deliberation, she decided to take the copper key and the mysterious book into her possession. She would peruse the latter back in the privacy of her apartment. These she placed into her shoulder bag. She stood a moment longer, ran the fingers of one hand through the thick, dark hair which partially concealed her face, contemplated her itinerary for the day, and headed out.

☼

Simone's shift in the ticket booth was dull and distracted in equal measure. She didn't feel right perusing the book which had been left on her altar while she was working, yet she was driven nearly mad with anticipation. When the workday was finally over, she nearly fell down to her knees and kissed the tiles in gratitude for her release.

Back in her apartment, free from distractions of any kind, she let herself explore the contents of the curious tome. The book was divided into seven chapters, each of which was occupied with hymns, prayers, supplications, curses, exorcisms, oaths, invocatory litanies, and permutations of divine and angelic names. Perplexing diagrams in red and black peppered the text. Stars and constellations which Simone had never heard of were propitiated and praised on nearly every page. Each chapter culminated in a grand invocation, a devotional petition as perplexing as it was profound. Not a single explanation or instruction was provided, nor was there any hint of authorship.

Simone was possessed of a passing knowledge of occult lore. She had paged through old grimoires and Kabbalistic texts and was familiar both with modern theological orders and those of past centuries. She'd always been inspired by the esoteric and the arcane, though she'd never quite been moved to undertake a particular practice. The book which she now held in her hands bore vague similarities to several texts which had occupied space upon her shelves at one time or another, though certain particularities set it apart from others of its type. While there was no shortage of indecipherable characters, the book contained none of the planetary glyphs or sacred alphabets with which she was familiar. The supplications and petitions were written in a rhyme and meter which resembled nothing she'd seen in renaissance or medieval texts, nor did it strike her as modern. The prose flowed and surged in a rhythm at once foreign and erotic, rolling and breaking like a tide on some unfathomable shore.

The final chapter especially captured Simone's interests. The whole of the section was devoted to the invocation of a particular star which was purportedly found at the southernmost latitude, opposite the pole star in the north. Subsections were devoted to the star's attendant angels, each having its own particular glyph and list of glorifying titles. The climax of the rite involved a long and complex incantation to the stellar divinity, followed by an entreaty that it "descend into the hidden chambers of the soul" of the operator, that they might know its majesty directly.

Simone read through the final section twice. Something about the rite captivated her imagination. She was enticed by the concept of a southern pole star, a secret monarch of the south that reigned invisibly while the attentions of the masses were turned toward the visible rays of the luminary to the north. The poetic voice in which the rite was composed inspired and moved her far more than did the often rather dry litanies and prayers found in other esoteric volumes. She decided, with little deliberation, to perform the rite such as she could understand it.

A modest meal of steamed prawns on a bed of rice was taken in a quiet restaurant overlooking a lonely cobbled street. The owner was a portly, balding man with a mild case of bibliophilia, too busy to afford the time required to seek out the literary treasures which he so enjoyed. In exchange for a constant stream of reading recommendations, along with the occasional evening conversation, Simone was entitled to two or three free meals a week, so long as the dishes she chose were reasonably priced.

Here, she penned a brief letter to her brother, Étienne, who was away at university studying music. Étienne was a pianist, said to be rather gifted if as yet unperfected in his craft. Simone had been jealous of his hands when they were younger. She too had attempted to master the piano, but with no hint of success. This despite the fact that, being blessed with ambidexterity, she had a natural control of both hands which her brother had to cultivate through years of practice. She enjoyed watching him play in spite of their sibling rivalry. He approached his instrument with a reverence which she quickly learned to emulate in other areas. She hoped to pay him a visit sooner or later, though travel of any kind was difficult on her modest income.

When they were younger, Étienne had been the only man alive to whom Simone devoted her undying respect. They had lost their father early in life, and their mother was cold and distant and inclined to intoxicating spirits. Though two years stood between them, the siblings had been nearly identical before adolescence bestowed upon them the distinguishing marks of their respective genders. People often mistook them for twins. They'd grown more distant in recent years, though still they maintained a perfunctory correspondence. When Étienne had moved away, Simone was confronted with feelings of isolation which, though they initially unnerved her, she'd since come to embrace.

Having finished her meal and dropped the letter into the post, Simone took a stroll along the docks beneath the shadows of the naval ships and mooring ropes. Her heart was fortified by the stink of the sea as she scuffled along the wooden planks. The gentle lapping of the waves against the concrete embankments and steel hulls soothed her restless spirit. The waterfront embraced her like a jealous lover. She returned to her apartment just as the sun was relinquishing its reign. Here she sought sweet succor for the soul, a preliminary purification which would allow her to perform her rite with an elevated spirit.

From a thick envelope of stained yellow cardboard, she removed a heavy disc of black shellac. She placed the record on a cheap turntable which she'd found abandoned in an alley behind one of the tenement buildings near the market district. The device was on its last legs, to be sure, but it had served her well enough for the better part of a year and she was determined to get as much use out of it as possible. Records could be played at 78 RPM, no other speed was operable. The stylus, however, had been designed for modern records, and Simone couldn't be bothered to seek out a replacement. The resulting sound, invariably, was just south of abominable. Whatever music could be teased out of the handful of old records which Simone had managed to obtain was nearly overpowered by the crackle and hiss of the needle as it moved back and forth in a groove for which it had not been designed. This didn't bother her in the least. She was content with the distorted harmonies which issued forth from the antiquated speakers. They sounded like the echoes of forgotten prayers.

She switched the turntable on and carefully placed the needle down on the outer edge of the disc. After the briefest of pauses, the resonant sound of a piano filled the room. Slowly, so slowly did the phantom fingers strike the keys. The bars of Erik Satie's *Sonneries de la Rose+Croix* followed, one after the other, like the peals of a church bell in the midst of a heavy rainstorm. The music had been composed for a salon attended by a group of artists, musicians, and writers in the late nineteenth century who presented themselves as torchbearers of the elusive Rosicrucian society. Its elegancies never failed to exalt Simone's temperament. She'd never heard the music in any setting other than her living room, but she could well imagine how it might sound in the lofty recesses of the symphony hall.

She listened with intent, allowing its harmonies to rise and fall within the chapel of her body. The melody, a slow march, announced its rhythmic phrases like the inspired utterances of a priest enflamed with holy zeal. It took four long minutes for the needle to find its way to the inner edge of the record. By the time it did so, there was no need to play the other side. The space had been thoroughly cleansed and consecrated for the work to come.

The ritual, when at last it was performed, was perhaps a little underwhelming. Simone read the incantations with great reverence, affording all the necessary dignity to the angelic hierarchies invoked. The climax of the ritual came and went with little excitement. A slightly awkward silence ensued as half-formed expectations withered in the stagnant air of the apartment. After a sufficient space of time, Simone simply closed the mysterious book and placed it on a high shelf next to a row of white-backed journals. She opened one of the heavy wooden window frames, seated herself on a bench which commanded an impressive, if familiar, view of the city, and slowly sipped a glass of white wine as she gazed out into the night. At length, she chose a favorite volume from her bookshelves and idly perused its contents before drowsiness overtook her and she went at last to bed.

Lux Æterna

Simone awoke at an uncharacteristically early hour, unable to remain fettered by the bonds of sleep. She rose just as the first rays of the sun were shining over the rooftops of the low tenement buildings which huddled in their masses in the quiet morning air. She washed, read from her daily holy book (*The Garden of Forking Paths* by Jorge Luis Borges, number seven), and made her usual rounds. The city's acolytes went about their affairs with a dignity and composure well suited to the magnificence of the day. The streets and boulevards presented themselves before her with the soft-spoken majesty which is commonly awarded to the woman of leisure. She had few obligations. A short shift in the ticket booth seemed to fly by in no time at all. The limitations of her occupation merely served to emphasize the complete freedom with which she passed her time. She embraced, with a gentle fire burning in her heart, the laziness of sunset, the open possibility of early evening, the hushed mysteries of nightfall.

Later, after no more than a few hours of sleep, Simone awoke bathed in the soft glow of moonlight which streamed in from the window opposite her bed. Several attempts to breach the threshold of unconsciousness followed, though none were met with the slightest hint of success. She remained exiled in the waking world. She attempted to court weariness by reading from Baudelaire's *Poem of Hashish* which, while not ineffective, merely dulled her spirits while sleep remained locked away in a place inaccessible to her.

She passed an hour listening to a collection of recordings of Armenian liturgical chants at low volume. She'd purchased the records for next to nothing at a temporary booth in the open market. Their covers were pitted and scarred, but the discs themselves were in fine condition, considering their age. She attempted to find the lowest volume setting at which the music could be heard (not counting the barely perceptible sound of the needle dragging itself along the grooves). She played one side backwards, for no other reason than to amuse herself, having long since broken the record player in such a way as to allow her to do so. She gazed at the faded characters printed on the labels. The titles, displayed in letters of faded sepia, indigo, and teal, were entirely unreadable to her. One of the discs had come with an old photograph of a holy assembly robed in lavish attire and gathered inside of a church. She was enamored of the otherworldly vestments, embroidered with stars and crosses and draped over the shoulders and arms of the priests with a luxury afforded only to the highest. Their altars gleamed with silver flames while above them hung a gathering of lamps.

When at last she exhausted the series, having played each of the records from start to finish, Simone was no more inclined to sleep that she was when she awoke. She accepted her fate, rose from her bed, which was also her couch, and dressed herself.

A stroll beneath the stars rekindled the enlivening flame within. She rarely saw the city during the hour before sunrise. The streets were filled with a stillness nearly unknown to her. Streetlights brooded, empty doorways languished in quiet repose, the very buildings slumbered. Simone felt as if she inhabited a secret city, known to few, veiled from those who have not passed, while awake, through the implicit barrier between one day and the next.

She wandered aimlessly until the sun came up and the city gradually came to life. Lights appeared in yawning windows, the distant echoes of alarm clocks could faintly be heard, bodies began to emerge from their sanctuaries and take their place in the unfolding of the day. It seemed to her as if the denizens of the early morning, being yet too tired to perpetuate the official rites of conduct to which society was bound, took refuge in an abridged system of subtle gestures and knowing glances which allowed them to conduct their business with a minimum of effort.

She found her way to the docks, where the rhythmic thud of work boots intoned a dogged paean to the rising of the light. The cheerful stoicism of the dockworkers presented itself as somewhat of a revelation to Simone's weary spirit. She wanted to fall in with them, to take her place in the carefree toil by which they propitiated the passing hours. She'd never wanted to belong to anything, never had she found an association or society worthy of her attention, yet something about the disposition of the laborers called out to her. Knowing well that she had no place among their number, for she was not inclined to toil, she was content merely to observe their rites and protocols. It was as if they were bound to a sodality through which they might preserve the unacknowledged virtues of their trade.

She wandered back to her apartment, determined to remain awake for the remainder of the day. She breakfasted on two eggs, scrambled, washed down with coffee fetched from a nearby café. The soft intoxication of fatigue granted a richness to her senses that was rarely achieved during normal waking consciousness.

She read Bataille near a window as the sunlight slowly swept across the wooden floorboards. The slender volume comprised the fifth in her series of holy books. Somehow it seemed to her, with a curious distinction, that there was more to the story than she remembered. The erotic transgressions perpetuated by the narrator of the book and his consort seemed to have expanded to include several incidents that she did not recall having read before. Early in the narrative, the two protagonists collected several tawdry mystery novels and combined their plots to fashion a mystery of their own. This they set about attempting to solve among the streets, alleys, shops, and offices of their neighborhood. In another episode, which Simone felt certain she was reading for the first time, they fashioned maps comprised of places encountered in their dreams and slipped them surreptitiously into the bins of a crowded map shop. She found the anecdotes intriguing. She couldn't imagine how she might have forgotten them. She'd read the book from start to finish at least twice before, and had not infrequently sampled its contents over the years. Perhaps it was the lack of sleep. To be sure, the forgotten narratives did stir vague feelings of familiarity within her. Perplexed, she put the book back on the shelf and brewed a pot of strong, black tea.

By the time the hour of her evening shift at the symphony hall approached, she was glad for the distraction. She'd resisted sleep all day, not wanting to upset her schedule too horribly. The evening shifts were short but invariably busy. The work would pass quickly. She'd stay for a game of chess then return home to surrender herself to the tender mercies of a good night's rest.

The performance, as it turned out, was not well attended. Ticket sales were few. A modest crowd milled about in the lobby before heading into the hall. During the performance itself, Simone shared the opulence of the lobby with Marcel, who worked the second booth, and Edmund, one of the attendants. The chessboard was set up on a little table which lay half-hidden in the shadow of the marble stairway which led to the balcony floor entrances. Large windows arranged in stately columns spanned the entirety of one wall, displaying a sky of darkening azure. The soft golden glow of the magnificent lights above provided a pleasing contrast to the onset of night. The symphony hall appeared to her as a bastion of luxury against the rolling clouds of darkness which threatened to envelop the hall from outside. Simone would plunge with relish and delight into the desolate wastes after the game was over.

Typically, if the program was particularly enticing, she'd stay for the entire performance. Tonight was nothing special: a smattering of Schubert, which, while beautiful enough to listen to, failed to excite her finer sensibilities.

The chess pieces were arranged, Marcel and Simone sat, and the game commenced in silence. Only after it had become evident that he was losing was Marcel inclined to speak. "You look tired, Simone," he said, his eyes glued to the board.

"Insomnia," she replied, placing a pawn in a perilous position. "I woke up halfway through the night and couldn't get back to sleep."

"Insomnia," repeated Marcel, raising his eyebrows. "Perhaps it's your theological temperament. They say Gnostics never sleep, you know."

"I've heard the same," she said. "But alas, I'm an unrepentant sinner. I ought to sleep the sleep of the damned."

Marcel, aware that his grasp on the game was slipping by the minute, pushed a bishop weakly from one square to the next. Within a handful of moves his pieces had been decimated and his king was in check. "As I don't yet feel quite ready to concede," said he, "I propose a variation on the promotion of the pawn. You take my king, but we continue to play. If I manage to advance one of my pawns all the way to the further extreme of the board, I resurrect not only my king, but my queen as well."

Simone was so intrigued by the notion that she was compelled to agree. Marcel's position on the board was pitiably weak, his remaining pieces were picked off one after another until at last his final pawn perished at the approach to the threshold. Defeated, Marcel rose and, leaving the remaining pieces as they were, bowed low to his opponent. He turned around without a word and made his exit. Simone followed shortly after.

Thoroughly exhausted, Simone slipped into the welcoming arms of sleep within moments of entering her bed, only to wake again less than an hour later. She'd been dreaming. Several images hovered on the fringes of her memory: the malice of unfamiliar stars glaring down upon a hyperborean waste; the entrance to a mine shaft guarded by fierce winds; a desolate tower standing in a place so remote as to have been forgotten to history. She got out of bed and sat by the window in the dark. Pale blue shadows gazed back at her with the monotony intrinsic to sleeplessness.

She slipped into a silken bathrobe, grabbed some candles, a box of matches, and a towel, and crept down the quiet hallway. The bathrooms in her building were seldom cleaned. Each floor hosted only one. She had scrubbed the bathtub herself the day before, so there was some hope that it might not be so desecrated as to be unusable. Luck was with her, it had remained more or less pristine. She ran the hot water, locked the door, lit the candles and put out the light. A single window gaped out onto the night sky from the far end of the room. The light of the Lesser Dog Star shone through the glass as she submerged herself into the steaming bath. She remembered, with some dismay, the image attributed to the star in Agrippa's books of occult philosophy. It was a maiden and a crowing cockerel—a fitting icon for the insomnia that plagued her.

Far from acting as a gentle soporific, as Simone had hoped, the bathwater seemed to bring refreshment and vitality. An unsought lucidity beguiled her. She seemed to occupy a liminal space between sleep and wakefulness in which unconsciousness, the elusive object of desire, hovered forever out of reach. She became dimly aware of the presence of some sort of monolith, a single column rising toward the heavens in the distance behind her. It appeared as if it were a blip on her internal radar. It might be several miles away, though she could sense it as if it stood immediately before her. Was it a tower? She could almost feel the depressions in the mortar between the bricks which lined the façade.

Further, at an inconceivable distance below her, she was aware of the slow and steady pulse of the invisible star of the south. It flashed and scintillated in the desolate abyss like the murmur of a wayward prophet. A quiet voice, barely perceptible, arose in response within the hidden chambers of her heart; a holy hymn to the continuous one, the ceaseless breath, the never-ending sigh. The stellar light, soft and sensuous, illuminated the naked cobblestones from below, bathing them in a milk-white glow as if they were translucent. Simone followed a sinuous route to the docks, slipping through an opening in an iron railing, passing through a thoroughfare concealed in shadows, stepping lightly up a stairway and onto an elevated walkway. The water level had risen. Quiet men transported unmarked crates up and down the gangplanks. A lush display of amber silks unfurled in the tenuous mist. Within their opulent folds gleamed the sacraments of oblivion, obscurity, and desolation. Hushed voices surged and undulated like the rolling waves of the sea. The waiting ports of distant harbors beckoned.

Simone opened her eyes. Had she been sleeping? How long had she been out? She glanced up at the window. The Lesser Dog Star had not moved at all. If she had dozed, which seemed unlikely as she rarely felt more awake, then she had slept for no more than a minute or two. She placed her hands over her face, fingertips gently massaging her closed eyelids. At length, she opened up her eyes and looked down upon the surface of the water. Strong and supple, it quivered at the slightest touch, sending ripples back and forth across the length of the tub.

Alert, clearheaded, and disappointingly refreshed, she rose and removed the drain plug. Back in her apartment, she gazed at countless darkened rooftops through her window. The inner vision of the southern star remained with her still, hovering at the limits of her perception as if half-veiled by a luminous mist. Disarmed by the persistence of the image, she turned her thoughts to other things.

She contemplated the contents of books which had never been conceived by their authors. There existed, deep within the hallowed halls of her own concealed church, a third order of the holy book. These consisted of texts which she had only encountered in dreams. They appeared upon the shelves of a particular bookstore, which, as with so many places which are located behind the veil of sleep, was arranged differently every time she found it. The shop would appear only after intensive, nearly desperate, searching. Once inside, it could not be mistaken for any other place; it was immediately recognizable despite its ever-shifting architecture.

There, she found books which she would have killed to hold within her hands if only it were possible. A book of palindromic poems by Jean Cocteau entitled *The Mirror of Hesperides*; James Joyce's *Abaddon*, a vast and nearly fathomless tome following *Ulysses* and *Finnegans Wake*; a slender volume by Andre Gide in which the perverse adventures of an amnesiac are recounted in a series of seemingly unrelated vignettes; a deliciously neurotic narrative by T.S. Eliot, alternately titled *The Rites of Babel* and *The Frayed Threads of Knossos*. Anything might be found in this place, and yet the books which appeared there were invariably of a particular flavor, a particular essence, they bore a sacred character which bound them all to the hand of a single, nameless author.

Turning to one of her bookshelves, she removed a slim volume of poems by Marina Tsvetaeva. Simone had received the book from a suitor who had been far too old to be courting her affection. She'd been quite taken with the Russian poet, if not with the man who had been kind enough to give the book to her. The bold and experimental lyricism did not quite reach such exalted heights as to qualify it as a holy book, but it was far from common. She flipped through the pages with subtle defiance, searching for a particular piece. When she found it, she reclined against a pillow which she'd propped against a wall, raised the book before her with one hand, and read with careful deliberation.

The poem she had chosen was titled *Insomnia*. She'd read it several times before, though its intricacies had never quite remained with her. She'd wondered if the poetry might speak only to those who suffered from its subject. She harbored the vague hope that a homeopathic effect might be derived from the text, exhausting the very mechanism which was keeping her so infernally awake. Perhaps if she embraced her lamentable condition, she might ravish it until it fell away like a spent lover.

The piece was an unmitigated celebration of the night and of the restless mind which could not quite lose itself within its recesses. Simone allowed herself to fully engage with the intricacies of the meandering verse, to wander deep within its folds and perturbations, searching for some trace of a key by which she might unravel the silken rope of wakefulness which bound her. Alas, the poet was enraptured by her inability to sleep, and sought only to delve further into its mysteries, to entice it until it devoured her, to drown within it. Any key found in this place would only serve to prolong her torments.

The exhilaration of the poet was mirrored in Simone by a timeless sense of tedium. This was not the tedium of fatigue, for Simone still felt wide awake. It was the tedium which is often experienced by those who venture to the extremes of the earth, where day or night continues unbroken for more than its allotted time. It was the tedium of arctic ice, the monotony of uniformity, the weariness which overtakes the soul beneath the unceasing glare of the midnight sun. The human organism, deprived of its ability to divide its time into alternating periods of sleep and wakefulness, very quickly abandons itself to a mode of perception in which anything that lies outside of the immediate present seems to become lost in the eternal.

Simone passed the time doing little of particular interest until just before sunrise. At last, she properly dressed herself: gray silk stockings, dark green skirt, slender peacock colored top with pearl buttons, and short black boots. With no particular plan, desirous only of breaking up the continuity of her exile from sleep, she stepped through her apartment door, descended three short flights of stairs, and set out upon the city as it emerged from the impenetrable dignities of night.

Simone sat on the stone steps before the entrance to the central library. She had reached the stage in her cycle of sleeplessness in which the waking world took on the quality of dream. Weariness was far from her. The barrier between inward and outward experience, which was usually distinct and clear, had become worn, dilapidated, and obscure.

Rays of delicate sunlight emerged from behind the rooftops on the opposite side of the square, gradually illuminating the white stones of the library building behind her. The heavy black doors would open in an hour or so, allowing entrance to the lavish interior with its dark brown shelves and reading tables, its palatial pillars and sumptuous wall-mounted lamps.

Simone enjoyed watching the denizens of morning march back and forth across the quiet city square. Their long shadows flickered like black flames upon the cobblestones. Every aspect of the scene which unfolded before her appeared to be meticulously choreographed: crows alighting and departing from surrounding rooftops, dim lights peering furtively from opening shop windows, a symphony of autumn breezes which held court within the chamber of the rising sun. Every movement, every subtle gesture, seemed to her as if it was a repetition of an event which had taken place countless times before.

Yet still the southern star pulsed invisibly below. She could see it in the back of her mind. Its radiance was fully visible for a fraction of second every time she blinked. It had risen from its place on the nadir and was now halfway to the horizon. Was it a messenger of the ineffable come to shatter the fragile light of dawn? The waking world had taken on the quality of an image projected onto a flimsy plastic sheet, its insubstantiality was as nothing in the face of the eternal.

Simone rather suspected that this was all a phantom of the mind. She was obsessive and suggestible; the idea of the southern pole star had clearly made an impression on her, and her sleep-deprived imagination had latched onto it. Nonetheless, its persistence irritated and intrigued her in equal measure.

Turning her attention back to the immediate present, she occupied herself with a meticulous examination of her hands. They seemed to be possessed of an uncanny symmetry which she had not noticed before now. If her right hand were somehow to switch places with her left, and each of them was mirrored so as to retain its proper orientation, would she have any way of knowing it? She vaguely recalled reading, perhaps in one of the antiquated medical journals which occupied a section of one of her bookshelves, an account of the psychological landscape of the hands and fingers. According to the article, the dominant hand retained the impressions of the conscious mind, while the non-dominant hand retained subconscious sensations. She looked again at her own hands. Being ambidextrous, neither hand was dominant. The sensation and mobility of each and every finger remained unbound by such distinctions. By the time she emerged from her reverie, the library doors had opened.

The library was currently hosting an exhibition of rare manuscripts and prints. The chief featured item consisted of several printed pages believed to have been penned by Sir Thomas Browne. Simone had planned on coming to the exhibit at the time that it had opened, but the spirit of procrastination had directed her attention elsewhere. She had read Browne's examination of buried funerary urns one spring and had fallen in love with the learned doctor. She'd spent hours studying *The Garden of Cyrus*, *Religio Medici*, and his catalog of imaginary books and artifacts. She adored his enigmatic and baroque prose, his endlessly inquisitive spirit, the droll humor which was largely lost on modern readers. He was like a holy book unto himself.

The pages were displayed behind the glass walls of a long display cabinet. Each page had been hung by a carefully constructed clasp, allowing the viewer to read the contents of either face by moving to one side or another of the cabinet. Simone submerged herself in the sublimities of the text. She read a detailed description of a method of cryptography involving the refraction of natural light through various types of crystal; a short treatise on the influence of God's angels on the slow formation of precious stones; an examination of subtle tremors originating deep beneath the surface of the earth.

Patiently, she followed a perambulating, yet elegant dissertation on the geography of the polar regions. Several points of interest were observed. The concentration and economy of magnetic force was examined, along with its subsequent effects upon the soul of the world. She read, with rapt attention, an account of the soporific effect of extreme cold on the human organism. Several cases had been reported, noted Browne, in which individuals so unfortunate as to have been made subject to unreasonable temperatures over long durations, but yet having survived, have told of a mystical sleep which they had undergone in which the veil of eternity had lost its opacity.

The depths of the lost work washed up like waves of ashen light upon the shores of Simone's ravenous intellect. She was stimulated and intrigued by a lengthy examination of the physiological effects of the songs of the sirens. Their harmonies, it was discerned, must occupy a musical scale that lay nearly beyond the reach of human ears, and which more properly belonged to the angelic race first created by God to witness His creation. Comparisons were made to the heavenly tongue, and further to the lost Adamic language as described by the Kabbalist Abulafia. The melancholic mystic was compelled to conclude that it was the perception of the eternal within the siren's voices which affected a loss of reason in the human organism. The unhappy sailor, having navigated within range of their harmonies, which were celestial in origin yet infernal in effect, was robbed of the will to remain in the temporal world, and would thus gladly surrender themselves to the abyssal waters of the open sea.

These speculations were followed by a study of the arousing effect which arises from the state of exhaustion brought about through continual prayer, especially in those cases where the ardor of devotion is so prolonged as to deprive the devotee of sleep over the course of several days. The long-term effects of excess sleep were examined also. The sources of illumination by which the sleeping mind was made to see while dreaming were then cataloged, there being three distinct types: those attributed to Apollo, Diana, and Vulcan. A fourth type of light was discerned as well, being visible only to the soul and comprising the source of the remaining three. This is the celestial light of which the substance of heaven is composed, as well as the light of prophecy by which the visions of Ezekiel and of the author of Revelation, along with several others, were illuminated. This light is unique, according to Browne, in that it might never be extinguished or made to perish, nor is it subject to the vicissitudes of time and of decay.

Simone was moved to a state approaching ecstasy by Browne's perambulations. When she had finished the text, she sat down at a table, the pale illumination of a reading lamp casting a numinous halo about her body, and simply gazed upon the spines of the several rows of books which occupied the shelves before her. There is a literary language which has nothing to do with words on the printed page. Rather, it consists entirely of the aesthetics of the books themselves, being endowed with the memories, contexts, and associations which we give them. From this ambiguous text may be derived secrets holy and profane, yet always relating to our inmost personal affectations. With no small effort, Simone tore herself away from these considerations. She rose, ran the fingers of one hand or the other through her hair, and made her exit.

Back in her apartment, Simone made yet another feeble attempt at sleep. It was no use. Closing her eyes only served to rouse her to greater heights of wakefulness. She tracked the subtle radiance of the pulsating star in her imaginative vision. It crawled ever so slowly toward a particular point on the southern horizon. If it continued its trajectory, it would rise directly behind the church which she had visited just a few days before. Remembering her desire to visit the interior of the church, and having nothing else with which to fill the vacuous hours of the day, she changed her clothes and headed out once more.

Having reached her destination, she paused before the wide stone steps. The icon of St. Peter gazed down at her as if to convey a secret sign. She was filled with a desire, as unexpected as it was perverse, to switch the keys which the stone saint held in his hands. She briefly considered the possibility of wrenching the book from his grasp and perusing its petrified pages. She wondered what great mystery she might profane in so doing. She walked up the stairs and gently pulled the handle of one of the two tall wooden doors. The door swung open and Simone stepped through.

For such a modest building, the church was surprisingly magnificent on the inside. Plush red benches sat like sleeping souls of innocence beneath ornate crystal chandeliers. Shelves of gold and ivory supported rows of flaming candles in brass holders along the aisles. A raised chancel of delicate stone faced the nave, harboring an altar of white marble beneath a circle of colored glass. Simone advanced along the central aisle, enchanted by the timeless air of sanctity which hung between the narrow walls. She took a seat on one of the benches, hands folded in her lap like sleeping doves. She bowed her head and closed her eyes only to behold a flat expanse of pale light, an unwelcome reminder of the lucidity that plagued her. Opening her eyes again, she gazed upon the altar. The pallor of the marble appeared intolerably cold, as if it had condensed from the icy breath of a God infinitely distant and remote.

She rose from her place upon the bench. A ray of light shone through the stained-glass window above, pooling like molten gold upon the immaculate marble. She traced the elegant carvings behind the pulpit with her eyes, finding within its textures the trace of dignities and virtues inspired by unimaginable fires. A narrow doorway stood to one side of the chancel, the door slightly ajar. Simone approached the opening, driven by a relentless curiosity. Prepared to feign confusion in the event that she was apprehended, she slipped through the portal and into a small sacristy.

The dim glow of a modest chandelier left the corners of the chamber submerged in shadow. A wide chest containing several rows of drawers lined the far wall, above which hung a wooden cabinet topped with an arched roof. A long white runner ran the length of the chest. Red velvet flourishes adorned the virgin silk, embroidered in a flowery motif, while golden tassels hung freely over the sides. Several deep blue cruets were lined up against the wall atop the runner, some half-filled with oil and others empty. A golden chalice and ciborium shared the space below the cabinet. To one side stood a double piscina of heavy stone, to the other an imposing black wooden wardrobe. The faint remains of incense suffused the atmosphere, slightly sweet and tinged with heavenly fire.

Simone approached the chest of drawers. Above the cabinet hung a painting framed with a thin strip of dark wood. A disembodied pair of hands, palms together, hovered above a rolling sea in the depths of night. A star blazed above them, stark and austere, its silver rays shining down upon the praying hands.

Simone grasped the knobs on the cabinet doors. She opened first one side, then the other. Numerous artifacts were displayed on three deep shelves. A silver box of simple design occupied the central shelf, while the shelf above was cluttered with several items: unmarked bottles, a pair of dice, a wax figure encircled several times with thread. Two small books stood upright against the back of the cabinet on the lower shelf, both bound in leather. Simone recognized her holy book, the black-bound *Kasidah*, on the left. 'That thieving little prick!' she thought, remembering the man in the cassock. A smile came to her lips. She couldn't help but admire his deviousness. She wondered where he could possibly have gotten the grimoire, and why he had left it on her altar. The second book was similar in size to the first, but bound in red. She took the book into her hands and examined it closely. The cover featured an equal-armed cross embossed in gold. Three additional crosses ran down the spine. She had half a mind to pilfer it, but for the fact that she had nothing to replace it with. Glancing behind her to ensure that she was still alone, she allowed herself to examine its contents.

It appeared to be a book of canonical hours. While the hours themselves were indicated in clearly marked sections, the pages had been left blank. Hand-written notes, meticulously composed in a tiny, nervous script, appeared in place of the usual litanies, hymns, and prayers. Several maps and charts interspersed the text. One particular map commanded Simone's attention. It was a map of the city, in which several locations were marked in red ink. The place in which she had left the *Kasidah* on the altar was among them.

A little further on, in a section of the book devoted to the morning prayers, a floor plan of the church appeared, wedged between dense sections of nearly unreadable text. The hand-drawn map differed from the true layout in one respect only—the sacristy was shown on the opposite side of the chancel. Other pages contained complex diagrams involving various elements within the church. The altar, the pillars, the topology of the building itself—each was thoroughly examined in regard to size, proportion, and materials. Yet further, weather charts and tide tables were sketched out in great detail. The paths of certain stars were mapped, especially in regard to their passage directly above the building.

Simone perused the hours of Terce, Sext and None, each of which contained several long epistles. Her desire to explore the book in detail was held in check by her fear of apprehension. Toward the end of the ninth hour, she found a passage which intrigued her, especially in light of her earlier conversation with the man who, presumably, was its author: "It is the Apostle's hands which mediate the light of the Holy One, each pair a different facet of that immortal wisdom. The hands on the right distribute the light among the hours of the day, while the left hands rule the hours of the night. Plagued by fires of wrath and persecution, beguiled by the cruel winds of night's bitter scorn, they have persevered throughout the centuries, for they are immortalized by imperishable essences. Their source shines invisibly from a house in the eternal: a fire of such profundity that it cannot be beholden by unconsecrated eyes."

Toward the latter half of the book, beginning with the evening prayers, long paragraphs gave way to isolated phrases, while the very last pages were left entirely blank. Simone was particularly taken with a series of cryptic idioms which appeared at the beginning of the Vespers section. The sentences, often mere fragments, were separated by compact ornamental figures painted in red ink. "God, that didst promise to count the stars by that word," was followed by "not the less I searched for the Unsearchable." "The glory of Innocence ruined" was found repeated three times with no mark between them. Several further idioms followed, concluding with a query which Simone found notably compelling: "Who is this woman who follows me to palaces celestial and infernal? Her countenance I cannot see, for she keeps forever behind me."

She skipped ahead, coming at last to the Compline section. There a single phrase appeared: "Faces, angel's faces, that ran before us in malice below the veil of the dreadful night."

Perplexed, intrigued, and slightly discomfited, she replaced the book within the cabinet. Her fingers paused on the edge of the midmost shelf. After a moment's hesitation, she removed the silver box, unlatched the clasp, and opened the lid. A polished stone of onyx, petite and ovoid, sat within the folds of a deep red silken lining.

She set the box down before her on the white runner. The light of the chandelier lent a dull glow to the surface of the onyx. She placed the stone within her hand. Its heaviness surprised her. It seemed to want to sink into the intimate depths of her grasp. Simone beheld within the stone an opulence which bordered on the erotic. Urged to explore its oceanic depths, she raised both hands before her in an attitude of prayer, the onyx held suspended betwixt one palm and the other. She sensed a core of emptiness inside the stone despite its unexpected weight; a bottomless void which threatened to devour the impure. She raised her hands to her lips and gently kissed them. "Lux æterna," she softly whispered, without volition or intent.

The vastness of her interior landscape was flooded with vision. A single star pulsed with empyrean fire against the monotony of an anemic horizon. The waves of a malevolent sea surged and rolled upon the desolate shore below. Simone raised her fervid hands yet further, placing them against her brow. A further utterance rose from her lips, nearly silent: "Somnus æterna."

Stone columns and obelisks, frail and diminished, arranged themselves in geometrical aberrations repellent to the human spirit. A ravenous wind beguiled an eternity of Antarctic waste. Bleached monuments arose at abominable angles as if to spite the colorless sky. Simone raised her hands above her head as if to court the breath of the Holy One. Her lips remained sealed. Her heart was pure as ice. As the stone passed before the fluctuating star the sound of shattering glass brought the vision to a halt.

She nearly dropped the onyx, startled half to death. Quickly, she slipped it back into the box, which was then replaced upon the cabinet shelf. She stepped out through the doorway to find the man in black cassock and skull cap peering balefully at the ceiling through bespectacled eyes. The circular window above the altar had been reduced to jagged fragments. Broken glass littered the chancel. A dazzling white falcon stood perched on one of the chandeliers above. The jeweled light swung gently back and forth as the winged beast surveyed its new domain.

Simone's presence provided the man with a brief respite from the minor catastrophe. "What on God's earth were you doing in the sacristy?" he uttered, his voice tinged with a hint of grave concern. The bird relinquished its perch and swooped toward the benches, spreading its majestic wings like an angel of peril. Rising back toward the rafters, its radiant body careened about the church on a precarious course. The man crouched to the ground and threw his arms above his head as candleholders toppled and feathers drifted to the floor. Simone slipped out unnoticed amidst the pandemonium, leaving the church and its clergy to the hands of providence.

Morning had given way to the ambivalence of early afternoon. A light drizzle fell from the vacuity of heaven, anointing cobblestones and concrete with a tenuous film of dew. Simone stepped lightly beneath the canopy of cloud which had gathered above the rooftops, seeking a hidden means of ingress to the secret places of the earth. She felt as if another city behind the one which she had always known had begun to reveal itself, as if she'd emerged from the waters of a visionary baptism to behold the world made anew by a fire sublime and insensible.

Exultet

As perverse as it seemed to her, Simone appeared for her shift at the symphony hall that evening. The prospect of sleep, by that time, seemed little more than an absurd hope, a flimsy dream half-forgotten in the all-pervading light of perpetual awakening. The shadows that began to emerge as the sun went down were scattered by the radiance of a dawning inner vision. A second set of streets and alleys appeared, their ghostly traces illuminated by the tawny glow of the interior star. Openings revealed themselves in astonishing places. Hidden byways exposed impossible routes which, though they were enticing, Simone avoided for their doubtful substantiality. The hours slipped by like water as she wandered from place to place. She arrived at the hall shortly before her shift was to begin.

Manifold figures passed before her as she maintained the booth. With unprecedented serenity she performed the venerable rites for which she had long since been ordained. Before she knew it the symphony had started and she sat facing Marcel on the other side of the chess board. They played a single game in silence as the eccentric coruscations of Scriabin's *Nocturne for the Left Hand* echoed through the lobby. Marcel eyed her with scarcely concealed suspicion. He doubtless wondered what she was doing out in the lobby, as she had earlier voiced enthusiasm for the performance and was expected to attend it. Furthermore, her game was curiously affected. She played only with her pawns, yet still she managed to systematically devastate her opponent's position until at last, apropos of nothing, she announced a draw.

She returned to her apartment afterward only to fetch the copper key from the niche where it hung in her cabinet. Simone remained for a short time within the halls of her building before heading out the front door. The harsh glow of the bare bulbs above lent an unlikely splendor to the threadbare carpets and the stained and peeling wallpaper. She ran her fingers along the rough wood of the banister, luxuriating in its chipped and battered surface. The inner recesses of the dour tenement building in which she'd lived for much of her adult life had taken on an unexpected air of sanctity. What had once assumed a face of dereliction and decay now appeared numinous and holy, the jewel-encrusted chambers of an immaculate temple.

She passed through the front door of her building like a star emerging from the mouth of heaven and into the ancient splendor of the night. Attendant angels of dust and mildew trailed in her wake, their musty scent redeemed by her delirium. The sickly smell of rot which had for so long lingered in the lobby assumed a fragrance of hyssop and jasmine. The façade of the building, chipped and crumbling and generally derelict, now appeared embellished with elaborate flourishes and ornamentation.

Simone set forth upon a route inscrutable and arcane, exploring regions of the city which had long remained obscure to her. Flickering lamps illuminated half-concealed openings. The ghostly trace of an arch shimmered with doubtful luminescence against the crackling paint of a factory wall. She passed a stairway, outlined in a phantom glow, which gave passage through a bank of concrete to a richly decorated cellar. Shadows glimmered in the ghost light beneath high vaulted ceilings. Windows without glass opened onto hidden drawing rooms lit by radiant chandeliers. Simone kept her gaze fixed on the southern star which blazed ever before her, no longer dim but now dazzling and resplendent, rising ever from the southern horizon toward the summit of the night sky.

As the light of the star grew in brightness, the visionary streets and edifices which were illuminated by its brilliance came to outshine their corporeal counterparts. The familiar stars and constellations were subsumed by its pale light. Like sailors lost at sea they were submerged, one by one, until the emanations of the southern monarch came to dominate the heavens. Simone wandered unseeing through its devastating glory, blinded by the light perpetual, guided by its insubstantial flame which now shone from overhead.

At last she came, through a nearly endless maze of phantom streets and boulevards, to her destination. The tower rose before her, a monstrosity of brick and mortar. Two heavy wooden doors rose atop a short flight of stairs. Simone produced the copper key from a pocket concealed in her skirt and placed it in the lock. It clicked as she turned the key and the door was opened. She slipped through the entrance and into the holy place. With a feeling of finality, she closed the door behind her.

The lavish interior of the ground floor resembled nothing so much as an antiquated library. Shelves of dark red wood housed countless volumes bound in leather, their spines bathed in the glow of open flames. Candles set into hanging lamps were carefully arranged so as to provide ample illumination. Flickering shadows played across the paneled ceiling, the decorous carpet, the polished surface of the reading desks arranged about the hall. An iron railed stairway spiraled upward before the far wall, extending through an opening in the wood panels.

Simone proceeded slowly through the hall. The spines of the books, she could not help but notice, bore neither titles nor decorations. The thought of removing a book from its place upon the shelves and perusing its contents produced a subtle sense of revulsion. She felt that these books were forbidden to her. Their very nature was obscurity. The mysteries concealed between their covers must remain forever so. The reading desks, and the chairs which stood invitingly before them, were like the serpent in the garden of terrestrial paradise. In any case, she was certain that much stranger fruits than these lay yet before her. The temptation to partake in this place was but a trifle.

She advanced toward the curving stairway. The wall beyond was unadorned save for an iron brazier set into a niche in the wall. Thin lines of sweet smelling smoke spiraled into the distance above. Simone detected a hint of putrescence in the complex bouquet of the incense, like that of overripe fruit just on the verge of decomposition. She put a foot upon the lowermost step, intoxicated by the fumes, the decor, the very quality of light within the tower. A threshold lay before her which she had every intention of crossing. Compelled by a desire inextinguishable, she began her ascent.

Quickly she scaled the winding stair, rising higher and higher within the enormity of the tower's interior. She passed by whitewashed walls inset with twelve tall stained-glass windows, all of them shot through with blazing light as if the tower was surrounded by multiple suns. Each window depicted an ancient pair of hands in an intricate arrangement of colored glass. Withered, rotting, blistered, and torn, the tawny flesh glistened and fluctuated as the luminous rays passed through them. Several of the fingers were broken and deformed. Some had been reduced to little more than bloody stubs, white fragments of jagged bone jutting through the severed knuckles. Others were so weathered as to be reduced nearly to pulp. Despite their decrepit condition, the hands appeared as if endowed with holy grace. The fingers, what remained of them, were flexed and arched with the vigor and intensity of master craftsmen.

Onward she ascended, passing the luminous images one after the other. High above the windows lay a final landing, beyond which stood an arched doorway which led into a further chamber. The upper steps, as she approached the summit of the tower, were inscribed with cryptic phrases. Each of them seemed to signify the title of a volume well-known to her, the contents of which were etched into the tenuous substance of her dreams:

The Abysmal Star
The Nocturnal Light
The Hands of the Apostles
The Keys Celestial and Infernal
The Imperial Watcher
The Immaculate Verse
The Imperishable Sacraments

Above the doorway appeared an epithet written in an elaborate hand, an indication as to the nature of the luminary who resided within: "Flammas eius Lucifer matutinus inveniat: ille, inquam, Lucifer, qui nescit occasum."

Simone stepped through the doorway into a lavish chamber decorated with furs and silks of every conceivable color. Jeweled animals stood frozen upon an ivory dais:

peacocks, serpents, stags, and other more exotic fare. The flames of elaborate candelabras glistened on their gemmed bodies. Reclining figures rendered in milk-white ivory occupied divans and benches draped in velvet. Their eyes gleamed with sapphires while their hands raised blazing torches into the air above their heads. In the center of the room stood a resplendent throne occupied by a personage of no uncertain grandeur and distinction. Horned, winged, and robed in a vestment woven without hands, the crowned dignitary patiently awaited the appointed interview with a decorum befitting an imperial official. Behind the throne, high in the far wall, stood a circular window unadorned with glass. The blazing star with which Simone had so unquestioningly aligned herself, the ever-wakeful watcher of the south, shone through the opening and into the chamber with a baleful glare.

Simone approached the throne of the shining one, the morning star, the unwritten flame. Deathless and unbegotten, the chief prince of the uncharted regions received her as if she were the most beloved of his advocates. A key was placed into her hands, which she quickly concealed in a place inaccessible, and a document was produced. Scrawled upon its surface was a name as yet unspoken. Simone added her own. Little more was required of her. She gave the customary salutations and departed in silence.

Simone feverishly wandered through the timeless regions of the night. She passed by towering edifices of brick and stone and glass and concrete, losing herself in the splendor of the sleeping city. Her explorations reached from the railways and covered bridges of the northern end of town to the docks and harbors of the south. The city's monuments drifted by, pale and sublime, possessed of little more than earthly splendor. The tide of light had rolled back. The night had been returned to her. The stars which she had always known glistened with scintillating brilliance in a sky of deep violet.

Simone made her way back to her apartment as the first faint line of sunlight announced its presence in the east. Wearily, she climbed the stairs, traversed the corridors, and stepped across the threshold of her door. She climbed, exhausted, into her bed, the new day's light streaming in through her windows. No longer for her was the sleep of the common. She had passed through her ordeal. She feared not the further torments of insomnia. She had been enlisted into the service of a sovereign power, and a sacramental sleep had been bestowed upon her.

The Apostatical Ascetic

The Doppelganger

I am an exile from an empire insensible. My place of origin has no embassy in this savage country, no consulates to which I might appeal for extradition. Denied the sanctuary of oblivion, I dream while I'm awake.

In the morning, still intoxicated with the last remnants of the opium of sleep, my attention is drawn to a silhouette framed by the rays of the rising sun as I traverse the passage between Praça Restauradores and Praça Dom Pedro. As the figure passes beneath the shadow of the Teatro Nacional, I can make out his features more clearly. Though I don't believe I've ever met this man before, I recognize him as I would my own reflection in the mirror. He's dressed neatly in a black overcoat, white shirt, black necktie. Thin tufts of hair can be seen beneath his wide-brimmed hat. A cigarette protrudes from beneath his trim mustache. Outwardly, he doesn't bear the slightest resemblance to me, nor does he seem to be the type of man that I am in temperament or disposition, yet I can't shake the feeling that we're one and the same, this man and I. We occupy two bodies, we maintain two separate lives, we're descended from two different chains of ancestry, yet we share a single soul between us.

I don't acknowledge my doppelganger, nor does he acknowledge me. We maintain a complicity of silence. I return to the solitude of the crowd and continue on my way through the narrow passage of Rua da Betesga.

In the early morning streets of Lisbon I feel as though I'm nothing more than a spec of living dust upon the vast face of the earth; alone, yet cast among the multitudes. Nothing that I accomplish in this life will cause the rolling tides of history to deviate in any way from their established course. Time will utterly forget me. I am singularly blessed with insignificance. My presence leaves no trace upon the world.

Grimorium Absconditum

I've had revealed to me the secret names of angels which don't appear in any book. They're part and parcel of our lives, yet we walk in their midst unknowing: the angel of the cigarette, the angel of the drainpipe, the angel of the ledger, the angel of impatience, the angel of the ceiling fan, the angel of ambiguity—there are thousands of them. They've escaped the pages of the grimoires by virtue of their obscurity.

The gates of heaven are not grandiloquent and wondrous. They are perfectly commonplace. We might gain entrance to the celestial palaces were it to occur to us to simply walk through them. And yet we pass by them unnoticed every day. They have no allure for what is human in us, they are impervious to our desire. Likewise, the keys to the kingdom lie unattended on the pavement on Rua Passadiço. I've seen them there, they sit in plain sight beneath a neglected balconet in a niche set into a wall. I pass them sometimes in my wanderings, but I don't dare take them. The very thought of the responsibility which would be mine if I were to do so horrifies me.

With these thoughts in mind, I pass into the safe harbor of Rua dos Douradores, where there is not sufficient space for phantoms or doppelgangers to haunt the modest streets and lonely doorways. I quietly step into an entrance bathed in shadows, slip up a flight of stairs, down a hallway, and into a hushed office. Without disturbing any of my fellow employees, I take my place at my desk by the window and immerse myself in sums and balances which are of no consequence to anybody.

An Empire of Oblivion

Sitting at my desk, the same desk that I sit at every day, in the same space by the window which looks out onto the narrow street, with a sliver of sunlight filtering in through the dusty glass, I sometimes allow myself to become so removed from what I'm doing that the weight of meaning lifts entirely from the words and numbers on the ledger before me. The symbols become purely abstract, leaving nothing but the trace of naked semiotics. Relieved of the burden of comprehension, the empty signs and characters become refined. I permute them and combine them, I measure and compare them, I place them in the alembic and distill their subtle essences. They become lighter still, until all that's left are dried out husks which contain no meaning. These can be read only through an abandonment of effort. They reveal to me the mysteries of sleep, of the void, of the empire of oblivion.

I occasionally find myself immobilized for brief periods of time. The strain of computing meaningless sums, of compiling reports and audits, or of filling out receipts results in a temporary paralysis in which I'm disinclined to continue my work. I desperately wish for a sudden epiphany of silence in which I might return to the primal emptiness behind the appearance of the world. If grace were to permit me, I would become an illuminated savant, an automaton of the Holy Spirit, capable of going about my day like everyone else while, in my soul, I hold court with the ineffable. But nothing of this nature comes to pass. The machinery of the universe continues its endless churn, the grinding of celestial spheres does not diminish them in substance or in essence. We have no choice but to fill the offices which have been ordained for us in the senseless mechanism of destiny. Before me lies an unfinished report which is no more or less real than the vestments of the sons of the gods. If I chose to leave it unfinished? No major consequences would attach themselves to my actions or the lack thereof, and yet the work must be continued, my fingers must find their way back to the pen and paper.

I wish only to be relieved from my insignificant toil. Just as the prophet Enoch was taken up to heaven and made one with the ineffable, I desire nothing more than that my own dim light might be absorbed into a luminous void, a Logoi of infinite silence. My absence would comprise a substance so fine that it would redeem the world.

Noah, Christ, Muhammad—these were prophets so unfortunate as to remain in exile upon the earth, forced to carry out nearly impossible tasks which will eventually be forgotten or misinterpreted. Having already brought to being a thousand fruitless efforts, I wish to simply disappear, to dissolve back into an ocean whose shores I have failed to locate during the brief time of my exile. I aspire neither to find nor to be found, but rather to be washed away in the unending currents of the Absolute.

The Mark of Exile

I take lunch in a café on Rua da Vitória. My soup is unremarkable, the very act of eating is little more than an afterthought. It is the café itself that sustains me. The dim light which is lost in the interstices between one moment and the next, the unoccupied stools and benches, the empty bar—these things nourish me with their simplicity.

Sitting at my customary table, gazing listlessly through the window, I spot another doppelganger passing by on the street. Again, this man bears little outward resemblance to me. What's more, he looks to be a man of action, having a temperament and habits which are in no way consistent with my own. We're as different as night and day, he and I, and yet we breathe of the same rarified air, our destiny is measured according to the same proportions, the kernel of our inmost soul is not entirely ours. Has the temple of my autonomy been breached? I feel no less alone than I did before. I have nothing to say to this man, or to any of the other men who share my true country of origin. We're little more than vestments woven from the fabric of oblivion. We conceal but a single soul between us. Those with whom I share the commonality of exile bear their tenuous existence like the mark of Cain. We recognize one another by this mark, this lack of substantiality, though we don't acknowledge it. When we spot each other on the street we turn away. We are, in anonymity, the last remaining representatives of the blinding snows of the extreme north, the luminous darkness found at the approach to the axis mundi, a place of pure, open possibility which leaves no impression upon the memory of the world.

The Mirror of Knossos

At this particular time of day, over the course of a single hour, Lisbon is transformed into a mirror of the labyrinth at Knossos. The threads of Ariadne have been laid so many times along these streets that they've lost their power to guide. The center of this maze conceals only absence. It's true—there's no beast harbored in this place, only disappointment. It would be infinitely easier if there was a minotaur. An empty space is left by its absence, a void of sorts. Philosophers, scientists, artists, and mystics have speculated upon the nature of this void, though as few have seen it for themselves, it remains a thing myth and rumor.

I try in vain to lose myself in the maze of streets: beneath the stone balconies of Rua Áurea, where the heads of lions glower at passerby from their stone prisons concealed in the shadows; up the curving slope of Calçada de São Francisco, where I'm taunted by iron balustrades and shuttered windows; around to Rua Nova do Almada, beneath hanging ghosts of white laundry flapping eternally in the wind; down to a narrow stairway which promises to deliver me back to Rua dos Douradores. Every day I set out on my excursion in which I hope to find, purely by accident, the center of the labyrinth. There I hope to confront the emptiness that vexes the city, and, in so doing, confront the emptiness in my soul. I have yet to find it. I know these streets like I know the lines of my own face, and even were I to stumble onto some back street with which I'm not familiar, the city holds for me no surprises. I have tasted of its fruits so many times that my tongue is permanently tainted with their flavors. I cannot lose myself within them.

In the course of my meanderings, I pass by the Basílica dos Mártires. I admire the stonework, to be sure, but I find no trace of holiness in this or any other Catholic edifice. Their god is too magnificent. The Absolute, for me, is not a vast and mighty thing but a simple thing, to be found in the curvature of an arch or the whisper of leaves across the pavement.

Back in the office, I can't seem to concentrate on my work. I'm distracted by the most insignificant things. A pigeon alights upon the ledge of my window. It regards me with vague suspicion, side-stepping away from me before again taking flight. I'm irritated at the sight of my co-workers, who all appear to be working assiduously. I can't bring myself to believe that my fellow employees diligently apply themselves to their work, day in and day out, as they appear to do. I spend roughly half my time gazing out the window, at the patterns in the carpet, at the slow creep of shadows across the office wall. Thankfully nobody seems to notice.

I turn within, closing my eyes, and behold vistas of great beauty and perplexity. All of the classical trances rain against my inner vision. Revelations and epiphanies appear like fiery stars which streak across the sky only to plunge back into an ocean of ignorance. My visions are magnificent, but they're of little use to me. They fail to release me from my condition of exile. I cringe from the vision of power and am indifferent to the vision of love. The vision of splendor has lost its luster, it lies tarnished and forgotten among a heap of discarded memories. I've lost interest in the trance of wonder. The vision of the machinery of the universe has broken down. As for the vision of eternity, I have yet to attain it. Only the trance of sorrow retains its hold on me. It overwhelms the ledger of my soul and immerses me in an infinity of ennui. The vision of mortality, they call it, or the perception of the futility of all effort. In the midst of this exalted vision I behold the very fabric of the cosmos: time-worn, warped, dilapidated, and stained with unsavory essences.

The Apostatical Ascetic

My inmost soul has been made pure by endless tribulations. I have passed through furnaces of torpor and indifference and yet remained unchanged. I am a true initiate of mysteries unknown to even the most erudite of scholars. I carry out my daily tasks with the diligence of a man who knows no alternative. I continue my work only because it does not occur to me to do otherwise. I find no peace in this, nor contentment, not even a brief respite from the irritations of the day. And yet I taste of fruits unknown to other men. I distill an essence, even while engaged in the most tedious activities, which dissolves the barrier between the waking world and the empire of dreams.

Beneath the mantle of banality which clothes the world is concealed an ocean of imagination having a magnitude immeasurable. A sunken cathedral, according to the lost books of the ancients, lies drowned in the depths of this ocean, a stone relic of primordial heresy in which the fracture between Heaven and Earth falls away like dust, and the gnosis of the midnight sun announces an eternal night of ecstasy and rest. Here is the hope of my return from exile. Within a hidden chamber in the heart of this cathedral, if only it could be found, the weary traveler might be reabsorbed back into the current of divine breath which permeates the cosmos. I have in my possession the key to this chamber, yet I'm not entirely certain that I have the courage to place it in the lock, nor do I know where the lock may be found, or even if it exists at all.

Lost in these ruminations, I'm suddenly aware that I've finished my work for the day. Without a sound, I rise from my desk and take leave of the office.

As I make my way home from work, a sudden crack of thunder shudders through the sky and I'm drenched in an unexpected downpour. I lift my face toward the falling rain. The water runs in streams and rivulets down the back of my neck, across the wide gulf of my forehead, in the lines which run between my nostrils and the outer limits of my mustache. For just a single moment I experience an ecstasy of innocence. I am pure sensation, freed from the tumultuous thoughts which assail me night and day. But then a horde of tiny irritations creep in, finding their home in the wreck of my body, causing my very bones to weary in the chill of the cold, damp afternoon. I wish to be anywhere other than where I am, I yearn to be a thousand voices never given the opportunity to speak. If only I could be something other than myself, I feel I could achieve the perfect combination of greatness and anonymity. I would be a ghostwriter for a multitude of disembodied poets.

The Citadel

At times it seems as if the invisible glue that holds the world together has loosened its grip. The layers of our day-to-day existence seem to peel back and curl at the edges, like wallpaper which has come unfixed from the surface of the wall, revealing a cracked and colorless plaster behind the artful arrangement of pattern and hue which we had always thought to be the true substance of the world. In vain do we attempt to fix what was never broken. We re-apply the glue and press the paper back into place only for it to peel back up again. Even if it were to remain dutifully in its place, we can't forget what we've seen. The worst of it is that we continue about our business as if nothing has changed; yet we know, we bear within us a flame of disappointment which we can never entirely extinguish. But disappointment can be a refuge for the weary soul. I have found true contentment in the monotony of autumn afternoons when there is nothing interesting to look at, when the sun is at the least inspiring angle in the sky, when light and darkness meet in mutual disinterest, when the colors of the street begin to fade as the shadows advance, yet before the rich, dark colors of evening emerge.

The rain has diminished to a tenuous drizzle, coating the dusk with a thin patina of mist. I trace routes well-known to the most common of the inhabitants of this end of Lisbon, arriving at last before the frail tenement building which houses my sparsely decorated apartment.

The pleasurable solitude of my rented room provides for me a citadel against the encroaching tide of night, the relentless roll and break of the waves upon the desolate shores of my mentation. How I yearn to drown myself within these waters! And yet I fight against them. I wish for nothing more than an eternity of silence, yet I hesitate at the threshold of the abyss. I'm like a soldier in a war which never ends, a war which by its very nature never can be won. I feel threatened at the prospect of my own extinction, yet I'm so seduced by the faint glimmer of eternity which I can just make out beyond the veil that I can't bring myself to tear my gaze away from it. If I were a stronger man I could kindle a light which is not subject to the ravages of time, and in this way ensure that something vital of myself remains in the world. This would leave me free to surrender myself to the Absolute, having fulfilled my obligations in this place of exile. It occurs to me that I may have accomplished this already, but that my own light is invisible to me. Perhaps my war has already been won and yet I continue to fight, unaware that the struggle is over.

At other times, I aspire simply to be washed away, leaving nothing of myself in the world. To drown under the surge of this sea would be the greatest honor I could imagine. No, there is an even greater honor than that—to be erased from the ledger is not enough, to have never tasted of the fruits of the earth would be perfection.

A Book of Tarnished Copper

In the evenings, I like to spend time with one item or another chosen from the shelves of my modest library. I find a senseless pleasure in the weight and feel of old books; their scent, their textures, the almost imperceptible variation in the thickness of the paper and the opacity of the ink. I don't consider myself a collector. I own exactly forty-seven books, each thoroughly unique. There's no unifying theme to my collection. I read mostly after sundown, and by the morning I can seldom recall more than the faintest trace of what I read the night before. On the other hand, I can describe for you the rich variety of textures found in any book upon my shelves, the perfume which arises from its pages, the feel of the book within my hands. I'm a sensualist even when it comes to literature.

Every so often I subject myself to the works of the Kabbalists—Isaac Luria, Abraham Abulafia, Moshe Maimonides, Joseph Gikatilla, Moses de Leon, and others. I feel that I am intimately familiar with their Mysteries, and have mastered all of their arts within my soul, yet I can't make heads or tails out of their arcane devices or cryptographic allegories. What's more, after less than an hour's reading I come down with a terrible headache from the strain of attempting to understand. It's both a blessing and a curse for a student to apprehend with the soul but not with the mind. I grasp the mystery of the letters easily enough, but apparently I don't speak the language. My tongue is dumb. If Kabbalah means 'to receive', I've received sufficiently but am powerless to transmit, even to explain these mysteries to myself. This notwithstanding, I feel that I must subject myself to the cruelty of these works, perhaps as an homage to the Kabbalistic saints, or perhaps as retribution for some forgotten act of blasphemy committed in my childhood.

The Ancient and Unchanging Night

I step out for an evening meal in a restaurant on Rua da Misericórdia. The food is uninspiring, the lighting hardly compliments the space, there's a draft about my table, and the waitstaff is cold and indifferent. Yet I can't deny the fact that there's a definite charm about the place. It has the appeal of mediocrity. Disappointment calls to attention the imperfection inherent in every aspect of life. It's as if the architects of the grand theater of the world couldn't be bothered to see to the details and have left ducts unpainted, scaffolding unconcealed, façades unfinished. A work which is neglected is infinitely more desirable than a piece which has been meticulously completed down to the last detail. Perfection pines for our flawed existence. Completion yearns for the incomplete so that it might find a voice therein, just as the traveler who's been everywhere wishes for nothing more than to find a place which hasn't yet been explored. A terrible apathy arises from the delusion that we have somehow tasted of every fruit, mapped out every city, deflowered every virgin. When we remember our astounding inability, our incapacity for greatness, our intolerable lack of true knowledge or experience, the world is once again impregnated with infinite possibilities.

I walk among the city streets at night and see nothing but crumbling masonry, corroded iron railings, and dusty window ledges decorated with wilted flowers. Looking within, I behold crippling inadequacy, a deficit of virtue, a void of character. Thus I know for certain that I'm beloved by the beloved. My very imperfection seduces the ancient and unchanging night, the soft light of the stars, the void beyond.

Back in my rented room, I find myself restless and irritable. Revelations borne upon the tide of night surge forth from the depths of my unconscious, yet I cannot contain them. I try to pen a few lines, but they come to nothing. The well of inspiration, far from having run dry, is fit to burst, but I can't find the words with which to convey the splendors which threaten to drown me in its bursting. My character lacks both the flexibility and the strength to give voice to the multitude of impressions that rage within. The mechanism of my mind strains, cracks, and nearly breaks under their weight. Oh the lies that I could tell if I could but articulate them! The real cannot be adequately represented by that which is merely true. I must find the means with which to express the inexpressible; a single voice is not enough.

The Temple of Sleep

My ruminations slowly wear me down throughout the course of the evening. Torpor dims the spark of living flame which animates me until I can sustain my thoughts no further, and I set aside my preoccupations and go to bed. I approach the temple of sleep and find that the door has been left open. The antechamber is filled with a warm and welcoming glow. Passage is prepared to the sanctum sanctorum. Upon stepping across the threshold, I find that I've been deceived. The temple is barren, there is no sleep in this place. I traverse a seemingly endless corridor of monotony and weariness, a timeless drift in the pale half-light of insomnia.

I'm disturbed by subtle perturbations which are not audible in the light of day. The machinery of night, quiet as a mouse for most, is loud and cantankerous to my ears. What's more, its operation is not continuous. Rats gnaw the wires, causing outages in one sector while others must work twice as hard to remain on schedule. The buzzing of half-connected circuits drifts irregularly throughout the cavernous hollows of the machine. The operators occasionally revolt, erupting in riotous uprisings which must be quelled by violence. Maintenance is a nightmare: sockets must be tested, batteries must be charged, belts must be replaced. Sleep is little more than a remote possibility in this place, a fantasy with which to while away the unending hours of the night. Eventually, as if out of steam, my consciousness exhausts itself.

Yet even in the silence of unconsciousness the pistons continue to churn relentlessly. Sleep is nothing more than a smoothly operating engine. Flywheels sputter without sound, flashing lights emit a radiance so subtle as to defy the visible spectrum, gears grind and scrape and nearly halt, slowing to a snail's pace, yet never quite coming to rest. Alas, the heavenly machine, the enigma of the ancient race of man, the immeasurable turbine of the mind of God: these are things which never cease.

I rise from my bed late in the evening, disturbed by the endless rattle of the eternal voice. A short stroll in the moonlight should put things right. I step out into the street to find that the stars have regrouped into strange new constellations. What's more, I recognize the new forms that have emerged in the darkened vault of the sky. They move in strange and unfamiliar cycles, yet the meaning behind them is as clear as a polished mirror. Everything I could ever want to know is laid out above me in perfectly distinguishable terms. I become as an oracle in the night, a secret prophet, possessed of the keys to the innumerable gates of suffering and joy. Before I can so much as approach the outermost gate, my newfound clarity evaporates. Without a single star shifting its position in the heavens, I find that the familiar constellations have retuned, and I can read them no better than I was able to before I woke. My moment of clarity is lost forever, if it ever existed in the first place. I beheld Truth for but an instant, and have now returned to the obscurity of the known. I give a sigh of relief and return to my bed.

The Invisible Basilica

Drifting in and out of sleep, I take up temporary residence on the border of the unconscious. I have erected a temple of the Mysteries in the tenuous landscape of hypnagogia. It is not an easy place to find. There's a tendency for the seeker to fall asleep long before the insubstantial architecture of the temple has been spotted through the endless expanse of cloud and fog. The temple has its guardians, to be sure. It's sheathed in a vestment of monotony and torpor. The way is not easy, and few will ever find it, though once found it promises a bounty of eternal rest. The Mysteries of all the stars and planets may be absorbed in a matter of seconds, the Lost Word of the Freemasons is here spoken openly, the Shekinah of the Kabbalists awaits the weary traveler within its walls. The Holy of Holies, beyond the iron wall of sleep, holds something far longer sought after than the mere Ark of the Covenant. What it is exactly I cannot say, not because I'm forbidden to reveal it, but simply because I've forgotten it. Once attained, the Mysteries of the temple lose their value. To behold them is to renounce them.

I dream of yet another temple, a basilica with impenetrable walls. Inside of this temple, though it is impossible to verify, lives the Angel of the Inmost Essence, the Beloved One, the Angel of Annihilation whose trumpet of brass causes the world of forms and substances to crumble back into the sea of naked possibility from which it came. I wish for nothing more than to gain entrance to this temple, and yet I cannot accept that this is possible. If entrance were to be attained, my vision of the temple would shatter. By its very nature, my utmost desire must be unreachable. If perfection were to be achieved, it would no longer be perfect.

Lost Among Myselves

I wake briefly, recalling a dream in which I'm a member of the aristocracy. I make small talk with important public figures at diplomatic cocktail parties, I dictate proclamations having consequences in various circles of power, I play the part allotted to me. But in secret I'm a poet, a member of a cabal of anonymous artists who pay homage to the ascendency of night. We seek to overthrow the light of reason, to return the race of man to its origins in obscurity, to submerge the shores of civilization in the waters of the relentless sea. Our struggle takes place behind the veil of sleep.

As I lie now awake, I'm filled with a vague sense of recognition for the figure in my dream. I'm certain he was another doppelganger. The secret brotherhood of exile, it seems, is not confined to the waking world. My reflections speak from both sides of the mirror, multiplied through an endless succession of frames. I've become lost among myselves. When I speak, I'm not entirely certain who it is that's speaking. What I have to say is of no importance whatsoever, yet I'm burdened by a multiplicity of mouths with which to say it.

Pneuma

I awake with the sun streaming in through my bedroom window. Dream images, half-remembered, emerge briefly, having no context or connection with one another: a fragment of a singing voice heard from within a railway carriage; a flowerpot gently tipping from a window ledge, just about to fall; a futile conversation in an office regarding a missing document. I let them sink back beneath the surface of consciousness as I get out of bed and prepare for the tedium of the day.

I stop for coffee in a café on Praça Restauradores, near an obelisk which is flanked by winged angels of black stone. I scan the crowds in vain for my unspoken brethren. I see only the faces of strangers pass by. Even if I were to catch sight of another doppelganger, I would be compelled to look away. This is the unspoken code between us, that we do not acknowledge our affiliation. Putting these thoughts behind me, I continue on my way to work.

Suddenly, having nearly reached the office, I find myself plunged into the midst of an unexpected gale. Fierce winds blow the hat from my head and along the sidewalk. My clothes are pulled uncomfortably against the contours of my body. It's all I can do to remain standing as I wait for the tempest to recede. Looking out onto the street, I see an umbrella fly from some poor woman's hands as the wind snatches it up into its manifold fingers. A tram rolls unattended down a side street, propelled by a cruel gust. The tops of trees are whipped back and forth as children take cover behind doors and beneath awnings. The brutality of the storm continues to increase. I'm swept from my feet and picked up in the gale, hurled above the narrow embrace of Rua dos Douradores, carried off to unknown abodes in the violent, cloud-enwrapped tempest. Here I learn the Mysteries of Silence from a hushed voice which speaks so quietly that it cannot be comprehended. The soft murmur of intangible winds initiates my body into untold pleasures. The very skin is released from my trembling frame. The bones are the last to go, swept up like dust in an autumn breeze and scattered throughout the trackless wastes. I've left this world of tedium and dismay, and yet my doppelgangers remain, walking the earth in my place, performing my worldly duties, fulfilling my terrestrial obligations. Having lost my substance, I cast a thousand shadows. They occupy every corner of the earth, filling its vertices with nothing of particular importance, performing duties that need not be performed. My multitudes are legion, my fingerprints can be found on every surface of every city in the world, but they are tenuous, brittle, and vague, and quickly fade to nothing.

A Perilous Ordeal

The House of Onyx

THE RICH reverberations of a gong echoed through the closed door and into the antechamber as if to mimic the monumental utterance of some forgotten god. A few moments later the door was opened and the shuffling of approaching feet could be heard upon the threadbare carpet. The sweet scent of incense struck Bartolomeu's nostrils. He was sitting, blindfolded, on a hard wooden bench outside of a banquet hall in an old, disused hotel. The hall, along with the surrounding meeting rooms, had been converted into the initiatory quarters of a society secret enough to constitute a household name among the local occult intelligentsia, yet too transient to survive the tides of history. His initiation was about to commence.

Bartolomeu was made to rise and was led by hand to the boundary of the sanctuary, where further progress was barred. The candidate was not allowed to enter into the Holy Place without first being properly purified and consecrated. This was done with no great ostentation with a sprinkle of water and the passing of a flame. The candidate, now purged of undesirable elements, was led into the Sanctum Sanctorum and made to kneel before an altar.

He was further bound by sacred oath, which was long and tedious and consisted of several parts, each of which was aligned with an immutable principle. The silence maintained in the period to follow was punctuated only by the swish of robes flowing around swiftly moving bodies. An object of some sort was brought into close proximity with Bartolomeu's shoulders, breast, and brow while sacred names were dutifully intoned. He was given a consecrated wafer to eat, along with sacramental wine with which to wash it down. The architecture of his soul was thus brought into alignment with the geometry of Heaven.

The Hierophant, expounder of the Mysteries in the inmost chamber of the house of the elect, proclaimed the themes and motifs of the ritual to come, his voice echoing solemnly throughout the hall.

"You now kneel in a temple not only earthy but celestial. The cake you have partaken of contains the substance of the flame which burns within the heart of the temple, while the wine contains its essence. The Angel Ratziel, the very utterance of Wisdom, presides over the sacrament. The Holy Flame must now be made to take its place within your own heart."

A second officer continued where the first had left off: "But be aware! There is a Word which has been lost, a Word most desirable. It is the formula which binds the Rose to the Cross, the Name of the Angel in the temple of the heart, the utterance by which you may take your true place among the Invisible College of Adepts."

A third officer chimed in, somewhat faltering in voice but no less sincere, "Find, then, the Lost Word! Cultivate the Flame in the Temple of the Heart! Maintain the Flame in Holy vigilance!"

Again the gong resounded, and the candidate was made to rise in the wake of its rich cacophony. There was a pause as the officers arranged themselves in complex geometrical formations. Astral lines of force crisscrossed the floor, running through the lamps upon the pillars, the holy stone upon the altar, the tips of wands and scepters as they moved about the temple. Again the voice of the Hierophant, much closer now, pontificated.

"You stand now at the entrance to the Palace of the Court of Sapphire, the Hekal Livnat ha-Sappir. Thus far, by work and by sacrifice, have you penetrated into the empyreal abodes. You are now to make your way to the inner chamber of the Hekal Nogah, the Palace of Splendor. It is in this exalted temple that the Word which you seek may be found."

Bartolomeu was led blindly about the banquet hall according to a circuitous route. A mystical effulgence suffused the space as the banality of the setting was left far behind. Holy characters were traced upon his brow in vibrant tongues of scintillating flame. He was led between the pillars of Hermes and Solomon as Earth and Heaven harmoniously embraced.

The lofty atmosphere was abruptly disturbed by a commotion in the near distance. The rhythmic thud of swiftly approaching boots could be heard out in the antechamber. With little warning, the doors of the hall were unceremoniously slammed open. Orders barked in German accompanied the brusque movement of several bodies. One of the ritual officers could be heard muttering something under his breath. A terse conversation ensued. Bartolomeu had little to no grasp of the German tongue, and was still dazed by the effect of the ceremony so far. It seemed entirely possible that the interruption was part of the initiatory drama. Unsure what else to do, he simply froze in place as the conversation seemed to escalate, the voices of the other officers joining in.

Within less than a minute, the tension had grown dire. The sanctuary had most certainly been breached. Angry shouts volleyed back and forth across the vaulted palaces of Heaven. The altercation continued to rise in severity until at last the resonant sound of a gunshot was heard, a thundering blast followed by the unmistakable thump of a body hitting the floor.

Bartolomeu felt his heart turn to ice. The sound of someone softly sobbing contrasted with the quiet commotion of several people moving about with the swift efficiency of a military operation. He began to shake violently, certain that he was going to be ill. Penetrating blackness alternated with white heat in surging waves throughout the length of his body. Before he could so much as remove his blindfold the world slipped from his grasp and consciousness was lost.

Bartolomeu awoke. The surface on which he lay rocked and trembled with a steady rhythm. He could still feel the blindfold across his face. His hands were bound behind him. It would appear that he was in a moving vehicle. The heat was stifling. Rough burlap caressed his face and neck, cushioning his head from the unyielding floor below. He sat motionless in the darkness for an indeterminate period as the events which had drawn the initiation to so unfortunate a close returned to him. A sense of unreality overtook him. He felt as if he were being submerged underwater, as if the sensations he were feeling were not his. It took no time at all for him to fall back into the smothering arms of unconsciousness.

Again, he awoke, this time with a jolt. He was in darkness, the blindfold gone. A piteous attempt to rise was met with sharp resistance: he would seem to be firmly attached to an unmoving object. Neither his hands nor his feet were free. A modicum of experimentation led him to understand that he was tied to the chair in which he sat. A frenzied wiggling of the fingers dispelled a slight numbness in the hands and wrists. The rope with which he was bound was fairly loose, though he didn't deem it wise to release himself just yet. Was he still wearing his initiatory robe? The lack of constriction of any sort around his knees and waist reminded him that he was naked beneath it. His feet were bare. His throat was parched. His body harbored a thousand minor aches. A distant creaking could be heard, perhaps the sound of wooden floors bending ever so slightly beneath pacing feet. A tiny line of light, barely perceptible, could be seen dimly shining down from above. He must be in a cellar near the base of a staircase. Was he hungry? Had he eaten? A gnawing vacuity in the stomach confirmed that he had not eaten recently.

Bartolomeu settled into his chair as best he could. He could not think of a single thing to do but wait. Perhaps an hour passed, it could have easily been twice as long. At last he heard the heavy plod of approaching boots. A devastating flash of light momentarily deranged his senses. A silhouette appeared, framed within the blinding glare. Bartolomeu resisted giving voice to his frustration as an attempt to shade his eyes with one hand was aborted due to the ropes. As his eyes slowly adjusted to the sudden introduction of light, a man in uniform and peaked cap approached. The cap bore the totenkopf and eagle emblems.

"Ah, good. You are awake," said the man in an agreeable, yet slightly patronizing tone. "You will be hungry. You will eat, then we will talk."

The man unbound Bartolomeu's hands. Another man descended the staircase carrying a steaming bowl. Bartolomeu allowed himself to take in his surroundings through blurry eyes. Bare concrete walls, some wooden bins, a staircase with an open door at the top—a luxury suite compared to the cramped apartment in which he'd been obliged to sleep over the course of the last year. He stretched his arms and wrists a little before gratefully accepting the bowl of rice and beef. It smelled far better than any culinary fare he'd been afforded in recent weeks. The second man made his exit via the stairs while the first gently nodded, as if to give permission to eat, before gracefully turning his back so that Bartolomeu could do so in private.

When the meal had been finished, the soldier pulled up a chair from alongside one of the bins, placed it in front of Bartolomeu's, and sat. "It is regrettable—the ropes, the cellar, the guards—yet it is necessary. You have my apologies for any discomfort you might encounter during your . . . let us call it your stay with us. There is a bucket if you need it," the man indicated one corner of the room, "to relieve yourself." Bartolomeu shook his head. The man fished a pack of cigarettes from his pocket and offered one to his prisoner, who accepted. A match was struck and within seconds the rich smell of dark tobacco filled the room. Bartolomeu was surprised at the fine quality of the cigarette.

"You might, with little effort, remove your bonds," the man continued. "The ropes are a formality. We wish to make you aware that you do not have the freedom to move about as you wish for the time being. Yes, for now you will belong to us." He indicated the door at the top of the stairs with his cigarette. "Just beyond that door a man is stationed with a pistol. He will not hesitate to kill you if you are so foolish as to try to escape. I have instructed him to shoot first in the legs, then to pick you apart in whatever way he pleases. I fear that you would not survive this. So you see? You will stay put for a time if you wish to live."

Bartolomeu simply nodded.

"A further meal will be brought down for you in the morning. After this, we will talk more." When the cigarettes had been finished, the man put both butts in a breast pocket and refastened the ropes which bound Bartolomeu to the chair. When the man had ascended halfway to the door, he turned once again. "It will be better for you if you do not remove the ropes. If you cooperate . . . who knows?" The lights were turned off and the door was closed.

Bartolomeu sat in the dark. It had been many months since he had been able to sit in a room by himself for any length of time. He had grown used to sleeping in cramped quarters with his mother and sisters in the tiny apartment which they occupied. A life of opulence and freedom from responsibility of any sort had come to an abrupt end with the unexpected military defeat. Bartolomeu, as with many others, was forced to leave his beloved city during the exodus that followed. Who knows what had become of his apartment and those of his sisters, or of his mother's house in the country. The invading darkness swept in from the north and almost everybody fled in its wake. It was as if a flick of the switch was all it had taken to put out the light of the sun. The national spirit was crushed.

Some relief was found in solitude. The simple act of sitting alone, helpless, in a place without light, was unexpectedly liberating. Bartolomeu forgot about the near certainty of death and let himself rest. At some point he drifted off into an uneasy sleep.

Bartolomeu awoke just as breakfast was being carried down to him—two poached eggs over dry white rice. A couple of hours passed before a man was sent down to retrieve his empty bowl. The soldier who had spoken to him the day before appeared shortly thereafter.

"Today perhaps we will learn some things from one another. But first, let us have another cigarette. When two men smoke together, there is a bond between them, you see? I would like for us to form a strong and lasting bond between us." Bartolomeu was glad for the distraction. He knew that he was being toyed with, yet he let himself take the bait. There was simply nothing else that he could do.

"Now, I want you to savor this cigarette like it will be your last," said the man after extinguishing the match and carefully placing the burnt out remains into his breast pocket. "Not that I am saying that it will be, mind you." He looked up at Bartolomeu. "No, I don't think so at all. What I mean to say is that I would like you to experience it to the fullest. Let the flavor of the tobacco linger in your mouth. Let yourself become familiar with all of its subtle nuances. A cigarette should be treated as if it were the body of a lover."

Bartolomeu nervously put the cigarette to his lips, looking up at his interrogator. "Go ahead," said the man, raising his own cigarette in a gesture of encouragement. Bartolomeu tried as best he could to pay attention to the flavor and texture of the smoke: dark and rich, more savory than sweet, with just a hint of harshness.

"Yes, that is much better than to simply devour it, is it not? It is far too easy, in these difficult times, to forget to take the time to truly taste our food, to cherish our sensations. Even in love we do this. It is execrable, this constant neglect of the richness of the world." The man put the cigarette to his lips and inhaled deeply, closing his eyes as if to relish the experience to the full. He fished the pack back out of his pocket and briefly studied the decorative image on the label as he exhaled, furling his brow in mock contemplation. He turned it over for Bartolomeu to see. The package was designed such that the top slid completely off when the package was opened. "It is a very interesting design on this package, don't you think? Very clever. A city surrounded by four walls, a central tower, a star above. What could it mean, I wonder?"

"Perhaps," Bartolomeu answered, trying to keep his voice from sounding terse after a few too many seconds had passed, "perhaps it's just for decoration. No meaning."

"Oh, but I don't think this is possible. It must mean something. Such strong images! Why these ones in particular, do you think?"

"I'm quite sure I don't know."

"I'd like for you to try and guess," the man smiled, as if delighted by his little game.

Another moment of uncomfortable silence passed. Bartolomeu studied the design. The dark red forms on the white background seemed to taunt his imagination. The city with its ornate gate, the minaret, and the stylized star all seemed wholly incompatible with the aesthetic values embraced by Germany in recent years. The star appeared on the upper part of the package, so that if the top was removed the star would come off with it. "Perhaps the tower might symbolize the unification of the city," he said at last, "and the star could represent its destiny."

"Ah yes," the man turned the pack over again and pretended to study the image, "that is most interesting. Most interesting, indeed. You see? I knew you would come up with something that would astound me. You occultists are so clever! Now, what are we to make of this?" He turned the package over. On the back was a broken seal, originally spanning the upper and lower sections of the package. The man pressed down gently on the top, so that the image on the seal could be seen clearly. It was a depiction of a woman, naked from the waist up, with one finger held to her lips.

Bartolomeu made use of his cigarette to buy a little time. "I suppose the destiny of the city is a secret."

"Yes," said the man, "the destiny of the city is a secret. But then of, course, I have already rent the veil of silence, have I not? I have ruined our little secret. Perhaps if we listen, very carefully . . ." The man put the cigarette pack to his ear and cocked his head. "Ah yes! I know what the secret is. Observe." He again turned the package over and slid the top up a little. "The star can be removed, see?"

The man looked at Bartolomeu as if he could possibly know how he was expected to respond. " . . .or replaced with another," observed Bartolomeu at length.

"No. I don't think so. Find for me another cigarette package, of a different brand, that has another star in the same place as this one. No, I think that the secret lies in the fact that the star can be taken away altogether. Say, perhaps, I keep the package but decide to discard the top part only." The man removed the upper section of the package and tossed it recklessly over one shoulder. "I have severed our city from its destiny, have I not?"

Bartolomeu remained silent.

"Now, whether or not destiny is a real thing, or if it is only imagined to be real, that is another question. Tell me, right now, what is your destiny?"

Moments passed before Bartolomeu realized that he was expected to answer. "Who's to say?"

"You are correct," said the man, "you cannot know. You may not live to see another day. But then again, perhaps you will. Your destiny is hidden from you, just as is indicated by the seal. But I have broken the seal. I know, even if you do not." The man inhaled deeply of the cigarette, leaned back in his chair, and blew out the smoke in an unfolding torrent over Bartolomeu's head. "On the other hand," he continued, "perhaps we have misunderstood the true meaning of these images. Or, perhaps, it is as you say—without meaning."

The cigarettes were finished in silence. Again, the man put the butts into his pocket and refastened the ropes. He bent over to pick up the top of the cigarette package before turning back to the stairs. "I am enjoying our conversations so far. We will talk more tomorrow."

Another night passed, a few meals were taken. It was late evening before the interrogator returned, judging from the orange glow of electric light which streamed in through the doorway as he passed through. The customary cigarettes were smoked in silence as the man studied the contents of a booklet. The pages were filled with hand-written notes and directions. It was a simple matter for Bartolomeu to deduce that the booklet contained the script for his aborted initiation. The reading was punctuated with occasional nods and several disapproving grunts.

"I think the contents of this book are somewhat familiar to you, are they not?" The man looked up from his reading. "Perhaps you can help me to understand."

Bartolomeu remained silent.

"There is a city," the man continued, "not unlike the one on our cigarette package. It has a particular geometry, particular features, and there is something hidden in its depths. The hidden thing is not disclosed in the book, yet it is represented by a single word. The word is said to have been lost. This is again like our cigarette package, is it not? Except that here the seal has not been broken. Silence is maintained. There is no direct mention of destiny, yet there is a task which is undertaken, which is perhaps the same thing. I must confess, this is far too erudite for my simple mind. Please tell me, what am I to make of this?"

"I hardly know myself." Bartolomeu's eyes remained fixed upon the floor. "Maybe it's a bunch of nonsense."

"But it is not nonsense," maintained the man. "No, I think that there is definitely something to this. I know of the Theosophists. There is more to this," he raised the booklet before him, "than weak Theosophy. I sense that there is something real, perhaps so real that I can touch it." He again opened the book and continued to study the script as he drew deeply from the cigarette. He exhaled with a sigh, letting the smoke pour over the pages.

"Now this city," he continued, "perhaps it is every bit as real as Berlin or Paris, only it cannot be found on any map. And yet it can be visited, like any other. It has history. The Theosophic view of these things is of no interest to me. I am only interested in the real. There are cities which have etched their walls and streets into the mind of nature herself. You may kill the people living within it, knock down all the walls, set fire to the houses, yet something of it will remain. It is like the cockroach, is it not? You simply cannot be rid of it." He drew again upon the cigarette. After a moment, he continued. "Now, what might such a city be named?"

"I don't know."

"You do know," the man insisted.

Bartolomeu paused before softly speaking a single word. "Jerusalem."

"Ah, but that is not the only city of this type. This you should know."

The pair smoked in silence as the man continued to study the book. "Here is something which I think you will agree is of extraordinary interest." He stood, holding the book before him as he slowly paced back and forth before Bartolomeu's chair. "*History*," he read aloud, "*has shown that the ancients possessed the means to keep a flame burning in an enclosed space, without the need for renewal, for an indefinite period. The discovery of lamps in ancient sepulchers, in many cases still burning brightly, has been recorded by no fewer than 170 separate authorities. Many of these references, in Greek and Latin literature, may prove instructive to our own art if they are but rightly understood. A lamp still burning was found during the Papacy of Paul the Third in a tomb in the Appian Way in Rome, thought to have been erected in honor of Tulliola, the daughter of Cicero. It must have burned for over 1500 years, and was extinguished upon being exposed to air.* St. Augustine claims, in his work De Civitate Dei, *that a lamp was hung in a certain temple of Venus in Egypt that bore a flame which could not be extinguished by either rain or wind. In Antioch a burning lamp was found in a recess over a gateway by the soldiers of the King of Persia. The flame was elaborately enclosed, and dated from a time soon after the death of Christ. A crucifix was found beside the lamp.*" Here the man paused for a moment, his eyes meeting Bartolomeu's own, before proceeding. "*Further,*" he read, resuming his slow pacing, "*a marble tomb was once found on a volcanic island near Naples which contained a vase in which the lamp was still alight. The light paled and was soon extinguished when the vase was broken. Pausanias tells us of a temple of Minerva at Athens in which a mysterious lamp of gold perpetually burns unattended. Khunrath, in his* Amphitheatrum Sapientiae Aeternae, *tells us of a liquid which burns perpetually with a bright light. More recently, a flaming lamp was found in an ancient Roman tomb near Cordova by a Mr. Wetherell of Saville. Let it be known then that the secret of this ancient art, though lost to profane science, is known to those initiated brethren who have attained to the Palace of Splendor. In that place alone may the tenets of the art be revealed, and this but subtly, for by no human tongue can the secret be passed on. Strive ever, then, toward the at-*

tainment thereof, and let the fruits of your work be confirmed by no uncertain proof. Let a light perpetual be established in a hidden place, without aid or instruction from the brethren of your order."

The man again lowered the book, turning his gaze to meet Bartolomeu's. "Is this not the most peculiar thing? A light which cannot be extinguished! I really must give credit to you and your occultist friends. Truly, you have risen above the common stock of humankind. You have conspired with angels to produce wonders that have eluded the finest minds of our age. I want to march into the office of Der Führer and tell him that all of our problems have been solved! Will you come with me to do this?"

Bartolomeu averted his gaze and sucked upon the cigarette.

"Joking aside, I do think that there may be something here of interest. How might such a light be produced? I would like for you to tell me."

"I don't know," Bartolomeu answered with more bitterness in his voice than he would have liked, "I wasn't able to finish the ritual."

"Ah, but we have the ritual right here, don't we?" Again the man raised the book. "Perhaps we might allow you to finish what has been begun. There are enough of us here in this house to do so, I believe." Bartolomeu fiddled nervously with his cigarette. He wished he knew what was expected of him.

"There is more here that is of interest," the man went on after a short pause, returning to the book. "There is talk of a series of holy rivers, of the heart of Microprosopus, there is a gate of tears and a gate of prayer. There is in all of this a truth of sorts, though only a partial truth. Much is still hidden. Tell me, why is it that you have become involved in such things? What is it that this provides for you?"

"I honestly don't know," Bartolomeu replied. He had no desire to defend the Order or its rituals. He merely wanted to return to his home and forget his involvement in such things. He'd been with the Order for seven years, having passed through several initiations, each of which had seemed to open doors into progressively deeper levels of truth and revelation. His regimen of ritual and meditation had been dutifully performed from the beginning. He didn't care a fig for any of it now. The immediate shadow of death made all of it seem like a heap of crumbling leaves by contrast.

The man stood and turned to face the stairs. He took a long pull from the cigarette, blowing out the smoke with just a hint of force. After several moments had passed, he turned again to face Bartolomeu. "This is not helpful," he said at last. "You seem to know very little about these things. You must have been a poor student." The man stubbed out his cigarette and placed it into his breast pocket. "I have not enjoyed today's conversation as much as I did yesterday's. Tomorrow, we will talk more." The man refastened the ropes. Bartolomeu showed no resistance. "Gaspar," said the man, pausing before heading back up the stairs. "This is not a French name."

"Portuguese."

"You have no Jewish blood."

"No, none."

"As I thought, yet you participate in an exclusive order having connections to the traditions of the Jews. For this alone, I have grounds to send you to a place where you will have nothing to look forward to but a short life of hard labor. This if you are lucky. If I were to have you executed at this very instant, there would be no questions asked of me. Not a single person knows that you are here. I only wish to know more about this Order of yours. One might think that you would show a more active interest . . ."

"Look, I really don't care about the Order or their rituals." Bartolomeu's eyes rose to meet those of his interrogator. "I can sever all my ties with them . . ."

"NEIN!" Bartolomeu was struck across the face with such force that both himself and the chair to which he was bound were sent tumbling to the floor. Tense seconds passed, during which Bartolomeu was aware of little else than the sound of heavy breathing, his own or the other man's. The sting upon his face, the chaffing of his wrists against the rope, these were negated by a certain numbness, as if his body were unable to accept them. "Our little conversation is over. You may spend the night upon the floor."

The House of Amethyst

Bartolomeu stands at the bottom of a great hill in the midst of a terrible wind storm. Clumps of elms and alders adorn the hill on all sides, thickening toward the base and extending down into a wooded area below. The summit of the hill stands naked beneath a sky overflowing with stars. The branches of the surrounding trees sway violently in the storm. A swirling chorus of leaves and twigs, ripped from their moorings by the force of the gale, careens with unconcealed ardor through the lush growth.

A man robed in rich violet stands in the midst of the clearing. Stark, white antlers protrude a considerable distance from the sides of his head. An ivory horn hangs from a cord around his neck, swaying freely in the wind. The man lifts the horn to his lips with the bell pointed skyward. A brief pause ensues before a devastating blast roars forth. The echo of the monumental note cascades through the tumultuous night, halting the stars in their courses and causing the earth to tremble. The sound of the wind is drowned in its wake and the hill is bathed in silence, though the storm does not abate.

Within that silence an angel descends, vast and terrible, cloaked in bright scarlet. There is a star within its breast. The wind increases in its soundless furor as alders are uprooted and sent hurtling through the sky. Distant houses are torn from their foundations and devastation is brought to the land. The angel has come as a tide of destruction, impenetrable and unrelenting, an instrument of holy wrath. The man with the horn has gone.

A name is revealed without a sound in the heart of desolation. The light of the stars washes over the scene before receding like an ocean wave. Not a single image is left in its wake. The angel has spoken and the vision is over.

Bartolomeu's temple rested uncomfortably upon the cool concrete. He lay with one arm agonizingly forced behind the back of the overturned chair, his shoulder pressed hard against the floor. Daylight streamed in through the open door above. The vision of the angel and the hill blotted out any other memory of the passing of the night. He had no idea whether or not he'd slept. Not a single sound could be heard from the region beyond the door. He was filled with an inexplicable certainty that the rooms above were empty. The very air seemed tainted by the residue of abandonment.

With some effort, and an appreciable amount of pain, Bartolomeu extricated himself from the ropes by which he had been bound. He stood, carefully and not without some difficulty, stretching his aching limbs as his bearings returned to him. Collecting himself, he stood very still and listened. Not a sound. He placed a foot cautiously upon a stair. Having detected no sign of movement above, he made his way up and into a modest kitchen. Half-open cupboards displayed their poverty before the slow creep of rising sunlight which filtered in through the windows. The upper section of the cigarette pack was found sitting on an otherwise barren wooden table, the star brazenly displayed upon its surface. He left it be. Cautiously he advanced through a doorway and into a junction. Immediately before him stood a small room containing a mattress fit carefully with a wool blanket. Sunlight streamed in through a window next to a small white dresser. The corridor extended both ways, to the left around a corner, and to the right into a room flooded with light. Bartolomeu froze, every muscle in his body tensing up at once. Not more than fifteen feet before him, next to an open door leading outside of the house, a man sat hunched over a writing desk with his back turned toward the hallway. The scratching of pen on paper could be heard, soft as hushed breath. A weathered pistol sat upon the corner of the desk.

A shadow advanced across the open door. Bartolomeu darted into the bedroom. Without thinking, he went straight to the window, which was ever so slightly ajar. He pushed the window open just enough to allow for a stealthy egress, and slipped out onto a shaded patch of grass before a thicket of poplars. Voices could be heard in the near distance, prompt utterances in a foreign tongue denoting the rituals of the day. A golden oriole heralded his departure as he slipped into the woods. Knowing he may be shot at any moment, he refrained from breaking into a run. He felt exposed in his flimsy black robe as he walked briskly away from the house. He had no plan. The single location on his interior map was the house from which he'd just escaped, for he had no idea where he was. The rising sun was at his back. Long shadows fell before him. His sole imperative was to establish distance between himself and his captors. He knew it would not be long before they'd realize that he was no longer in the cellar.

After an hour or more of brisk walking, Bartolomeu allowed himself a furtive glance behind. He almost expected to see his interrogator, playfully following along as if his escape were part of an elaborate game of cat and mouse. Nothing but the undisturbed tranquility of the woods extended behind him. He pushed on, losing himself in the vastness of the natural world.

The uncertainty of his situation lent a lightness to his step. The fatality of a truly fruitless endeavor, so he began to understand, can bring with it a peculiar sense of freedom. He was as ready to die as he was to live. He felt no need to bother himself over particularities, better to cast himself without reserve onto the uncharted waters of fate. No inner compass seemed to guide him, no destination beckoned. Something seemed to have come unbound within him during his time in the cellar. He found himself content to simply wander through the unfamiliar landscape, unhampered by hope or trepidation.

Dark trunks rose like sentinels before him in an eternal court of emerald and jade. Shifting shadows lay like sticks of yarrow cast upon the floor of some lost temple. Bartolomeu pushed further on into the heart of the wood, protected from the rays of the blazing sun by a canopy of leaves and interlocking branches. A sort of giddiness overcame him. The beauty of the place helped ward off his anticipation of pursuit or capture. His very lack of power soothed him. Let them come, he thought. What could I possibly do to stop them?

The further he marched through the woods along the passage of the sun, the more his spirits rose. He made his way through tight, mossy enclosures and over the rot of fallen wood. Stately palaces enwrapped in ivy gripped the earth in topographical conspiracies as a tapestry of jewels unfolded at his feet. The forest described for him a secret cartography of the soul. The verdant landscape appeared as a mirror in which the tangled trunks and interlacing boughs traced venerable routes long familiar to him. It was as if they comprised the convoluted streams of a rich family history newly revealed, yet known innately by the very blood which flowed through his veins. Their quiet truth confessed its ancient protocols, their mysteries never questioned, their emanations never failing to strike the hidden chambers of his heart. Nature's temple placed him on a throne unmoving, ever present.

He walked for hours without rest, his robe occasionally snagging on protruding twigs or brambles. He found a mausoleum hidden deep in the heart of the wood. The impressive stone façade stood before a wide clearing. Its straight edges and peaked roof seemed to harbor a quiet defiance against the irregularity of the natural world. Its ornamental flourishes caught the shifting sunlight with a stately grace.

Bartolomeu traversed the rounded steps before the entrance to the tomb. Artful arrangements of heavy stone sheltered three archways, each inset with an imposing iron door. The central arch dominated, while the two to either side stood back a way as if crouching in the shadows. Bronze plaques graced the doors. Unpolished and green with oxidation, they displayed the names and stations of the deceased.

Bartolomeu placed a hand upon the rough wall. The monument seemed, upon his touch, to emit an elemental force. He sat in the shade of the larger of the arches, allowing himself to rest against a corner where iron met with stone. A restful ease overtook him. He closed his eyes, letting his thoughts drift. Images flitted playfully across the theater of the senses. He found himself contemplating the layout of a family estate on the outskirts of Paris (now in the occupied zone, which for all he knew he was currently in the heart of). The estate was owned by his grandfather on the French side of the family. A modestly successful law practice allowed him to maintain the estate, which, to Bartolomeu's young eyes, had appeared vast and full of wonder. When his grandfather passed away, shortly after his grandmother had herself succumbed to the ravages of age, and the estate was sold, a portion of the proceeds were put into a trust which allowed Bartolomeu to lead the life of a dilettante.

The events of one particular afternoon seemed to beckon to him from across the void. He could not have been any older than five or six. He'd been left to explore the lavish interior of the estate on his own while the adults sipped claret in the garden and his sisters played in the water fountain. He'd managed to stumble upon a chamber in the downstairs area of the house, below ground level, that he had never been inside before. It was his grandfather's private office, the door to which was usually kept firmly locked. Bartolomeu entered the forbidden room with a reverence granted only to young children who are faced with something of the adult world which they cannot fully comprehend. Shelves of rich dark wood lined the walls, replete with the fading spines of old books and the occasional miniature globe. The walls themselves were papered with a Moroccan design in enticing shades of honey and jade. Taxidermy appeared in auspicious places: the head of a majestic tiger extended from a wooden plaque above the heavy writing desk, a peacock occupied one shadowy corner beneath the unlit bulb of a stylish standing lamp, a hare stood perched on an iron stand upon a shelf. A large bulb beneath a ceiling fan cast a pleasant yellow-orange glow across the miraculous décor and the pungent smell of rich tobacco infused the atmosphere. More than anything, the intoxicating space perfectly resembled his grandfather, as if it had somehow been composed of the essence of the man. Bartolomeu felt that he would have no trouble identifying the denizen of the room even if he'd stumbled across it in some strange house in a neighborhood unknown to him. He was strongly affected by the notion that a space might bear such a strong imprint of a person's character. It was the echo of this affectation that gripped him as he came back to his senses.

He opened his eyes. Some time had passed. The sun had well begun its descent, its light gleaming from the leafy treetops high above. He rose to his feet, compelled to push on further toward his unknown destination. He made his way down the wide stone steps, circled around to the back of the mausoleum, and disappeared into a thick cluster of oaks.

Darkening shadows suffused the wood with a fragrance of oblivion as night descended on the back of the sinking sun. Bartolomeu followed a subtle but persistent inclination to head vaguely northward through the undergrowth. He wondered briefly about his fellow initiates in the Order. Were they still alive? At least one of them seemed to have fallen when the initiation was interrupted. He felt a curious detachment from it all, as if the events of the preceding days had happened to another person. Would the gravity of what he had undergone catch up with him? Would he be overcome with grief or fear? It seemed a matter of little importance to him now.

Several hours must have passed. It had become quite dark. Bartolomeu's body was drenched with fatigue, though this hardly bothered him. He was hopelessly lost and had not the slightest clue where he was going, yet he exulted in his pitiable circumstance. He simply could not bring himself to register the slightest bit of concern for his own welfare. It was as if he had become a ghost, set free from the conditions which enfetter the human spirit, stripped of the titles and honors by which his place was established in a world where he had never felt at home. He drifted freely from one wonder to the next, content merely to continue through the wilderness.

He wandered onto a broad, cultivated footpath. After a short distance the trees began to thin, opening at length onto a paved road extending in either direction perpendicular to the path. In the near distance the road came to a head before a modest, two-story manor cradled in moonlight. A white-painted brick façade harbored several identical windows above and to the sides of a stately doorway framed by unadorned white pillars. An iron-railed balcony sat above the entrance, topped by a pair of closed glass doors. The front garden had succumbed to an overgrowth of weeds, otherwise the house looked fairly pristine. Bartolomeu approached the door. He paused before knocking, admiring the austerity of the design. It was as if the manor bore a uniform betokening an office of understated importance. It was quaint, yet somehow regal at the same time.

Bartolomeu's knock was a formality. He felt a certainty within his heart that the manor was uninhabited. Nor did he feel any guilt at the prospect of making use of the establishment as a resting place for the night. It seemed to him to be as much a feature of the natural world as anything else. He wasn't even surprised to find the front door unlocked, though he'd been prepared to enter by force if need be.

He stepped into a dark, expansive foyer enclosed in wood-paneled walls. A wide staircase occupied one side, extending to a railed balustrade which encircled the inner boundary of an upper story. The flick of a switch suffused the room with a soft orange glow from a bulbous chandelier above. The manor seemed to come alive in the light, as if it had been woken from a long and heavy sleep. A thin layer of dust covered everything, from the ivory fireplace to the delicate jade vases that sat on little end-tables on either side of the staircase. A divan before the fireplace was uncovered. A quick investigation revealed that the furniture in some of the surrounding rooms was in the same state. He was given the impression that the occupants had left in a hurry.

Bartolomeu ascended the staircase as if it were his own. He went straight into a little bedroom on the upper floor, considered climbing into the bed, thought better of it, and again descended to the main floor to sleep on the divan. He slept on his back beneath the soft glow of the chandelier. As he drifted toward unconsciousness, he imagined that he lay within a holy chancel in the heart of the sun.

The House of Pearl

Bartolomeu dreamt of clandestine missives passing from the hands of shadowy ensigns to those of gentlemen of un-official influence, a hidden chamber deep within the heart of the embassy of some unknown country, a notary with wings who spoke in codes comprised of cartographical notation, and a school of architectural mysteries perpetu-ated in secret throughout the ages. At one point he found himself looking down upon the manor from above. A spotted leopard slept before the entryway. A sudden light dimly illuminated the darkened house. The light flickered upon the windowpanes as if each room housed but a single flame. Incandescent geometric patterns darted and flashed across the glass in complex permutations. The sleeping leopard woke, raised her head, sniffed the air. She rose and nudged the front door open with her nose. In she went, and the house became as if translucent. Bartolomeu could make out the contours of every room from his vantage point above, each of them illuminated by candlelight. One room only remained unlit, though he couldn't get a clear impression as to its precise location.

Upon waking, he began to explore the manor. Its ex-pansive layout provided plenty of intriguing features with which to keep him occupied. He had grown used to far more austere environments in recent years. In some regard it reminded him of his grandfather's estate, if for no other reason than that it provided him with an abundance of well-furnished spaces to investigate. Nothing he encountered exceeded the bounds of modest taste, yet it was clear that the occupants had no shortage of disposable wealth. He briefly searched for a more suitable set of clothes, but found nothing even remotely in his size. In any case, he wasn't sure how comfortable he would be dressing in another man's wardrobe. By now his robe was tattered and the fringes were caked with filth, but he felt comfortable enough within it. He wore it like a uniform.

Every section of the manor was found to harbor items of exquisite interest. In a bedroom on the upper floor, he found a clock set into a hexagonal box of dark, polished wood. The open lid was inset with a circle of brass engraved with the image of a tortoise. The venerable creature, curiously, bore a flaming candle upon its back. He wondered at the unusual workmanship. He imagined that the tortoise inhabited an irrigated enclosure beneath the manor grounds, casting strange shadows as it made its way from place to place among the foundations of the house.

In a parlor, located on the ground floor, he found a little stand on which resided a statue of an owl in polished silver. The solemnity with which the bird surveyed its domain cast a spell of sorts upon the room. He held the statue in his hands, surprised at its weight. Where might one purchase such a curio, he wondered? The place was filled with things of which Bartolomeu had never seen the like before.

Elsewhere he stumbled upon a curious map of a city which didn't seem to exist. It was etched in a copper plate set into the surface of a writing desk, just above the pad, in one of the two libraries. The legend bore the title "Adocentyn." Bartolomeu traced the streets and alleyways with the fingers of one hand, delighting in the intricacy of the design. Torches lit stone staircases which descended into unknown darknesses, gates were topped with images of the heads of animals, footbridges spanned narrow byways connecting one building to the next—every section of the city was rendered in meticulous detail.

A second library contained two tall bookshelves filled entirely with thick, untitled volumes containing maps of every major city in the world, all arranged in chronological order, spanning from ancient times to the present day. Bartolomeu wondered if one of the inhabitants had been a cartographer, though he found no certain evidence one way or another. In point of fact, without stooping to indecent acts of intrusion, he found very little to indicate any details at all pertaining to the lives of the previous occupants of the manor.

As the days passed, Bartolomeu grew increasingly at home in his new habitations. Hunger was not a problem. A reasonable cache of unspoiled food was found in the pantry. There was an endless supply of white rice, pasta noodles, and several jars of jam, along with honey, salt, sugar and oats. An abundance of aged wine was found stockpiled in a cellar, to which he helped himself, if only in moderation.

Bartolomeu allowed his sleeping schedule to be determined by the fickle winds of fancy. When he was young he had spent a perfectly sublime six weeks deeply involved in a love affair with a girl who worked behind the counter of a local post office. He'd become increasingly enamored with her in the weeks prior to their dalliance. Nearly every day he found some reason to send a parcel so that he could talk with her. Finally, weary of awaiting his advances, the girl insisted that he take her by the wrist, march her back to his apartment, and make fervent and impassioned love to her.

The days and nights to follow drifted by in a luxurious haze. The girl quit her job at the post office. Bartolomeu himself had no obligations on his time. The happy couple abandoned all traces of responsibility in order to devote themselves entirely to the indulgence of their appetites. A veil was rent asunder in the house of pleasure, the sacred shared its mysteries with the profane. No schedule could bind the lovers. The stations of the sun and moon existed purely for their amusement. Often they would wander the streets late at night, hand in hand or with their arms around each other's waists, without the slightest care or destination, eager only to return to the apartment and satisfy each other's passions. Forays into the light of day were undertaken only in order to procure coffee and pastries, steamed prawns and fresh water chestnuts, or whatever else might satiate their desire of the moment.

Within a month, the flames had cooled. Restlessness set in. Their ardor became tepid, and their bonds dissolved. They saw less and less of each other. The girl took a job in an architectural firm and ended up marrying a journalist who wrote for a reactionary paper. Bartolomeu pursued his interests in other directions. He never forgot his half-season of carefree bliss. He often yearned for its return, if not so much for the person with whom he had spent it.

The same feeling came back to him in the manor. It was as if he had immersed himself within the waters of abandonment and entered into an amorous engagement with something so intangible that it proved to be ubiquitous. The passage of time once again lost any trace of meaning. Sleep was taken when and where it might occur to him to take it. His temporary residence was graced with a sense of the eternal.

Knowing the possibility that the original occupants of the manor would eventually return, he took care to avoid disturbing the furnishings overmuch. This notwithstanding, the place had undergone a marked change since he had taken up residency within its walls. The change was subtle, though the effects thereof appeared as clear as day to Bartolomeu's inner eye. A reorientation of sorts would seem to have occurred. The very atmosphere had been refined. A steady pulse in the astral light bespoke a holy elevation, the attainment of a royal office. It was as if the earthly manor had somehow become reconciled with its counterpart in the invisible.

Fresh mysteries made themselves apparent in every nook and corner. Geometrical revelations were discerned in the dimensions between balconies and window frames, arches and awnings. The angle of the sunlight streaming in through the windows at certain stations of the day traced epiphanic symphonies upon the patterns on the carpets and the polished wood of the paneled walls. Bartolomeu defined a sacred alphabet in his meanderings from room to room, from winding stair to vaulted corridor, his every move a sacred gesture in some elaborate rite by which the talismanic body of the manor might be sanctified.

In the depths of the night the house became a habitation for untold hordes of holy living spirits. Brilliant beings of scintillating flame coursed up and down the corridors, leaving trails of luminescent ether in their wake. A troupe of

Tarshishim marched in the half-light of the parlor, tracing elaborate processions in which could be read the signature of Adam. Seraphs strode the balustrade which lined the upper floors, while the Kerubim held congregations in the stairwells and the servant's quarters. They departed back to their abodes and habitations as the sun came up, making way for the sparkling austerity of daylight. Bartolomeu paid them little mind, pausing briefly only to give a solemn sign of sanctity as he passed by them.

Having mapped the layout of the manor in his mind, it soon became apparent that there existed a space not accounted for. There was a room, so he determined, somewhere in the heart of the house, presumably between the two libraries, that had not yet been explored. Fruitlessly he searched. He fingered the undersides of moldings and the decorated surfaces of every corner block that he could locate, hoping to find somewhere a secret catch. Bookshelves were nudged just slightly, enough to see if they might shelter a hidden opening. The insides of the fireplaces were thoroughly searched, the cellars probed and the pantry cupboards inspected—all to no avail. Several days after he had given up his search he noticed a curious irregularity in the pattern of the wallpaper in the southernmost library. A vertical section of the design, located just behind the writing desk, seemed to deviate slightly from that displayed in the remaining parts of the room. The inconsistency only applied to a small area, located about chest-height. Upon a careful examination of the design, Bartolomeu found that the floral pattern, an assembly of stems and bells in flat blue on white, was reversed over a single iteration of the arrangement. He ran his fingers along the delicate curves and flourishes. A shallow depression was encountered midway down the length of a curving stalk. There was an audible 'click' in the near distance, the exact location of which was obscured by the acoustics of the room. A modicum of investigation revealed a square of wood paneling, located in the hallway just outside the library, which protruded just a little from the wall. The square was trivial to remove. Behind it was a tiny space about the length of two small closets. Wooden panels in the exact same style lined the walls, and a door stood closed at the far end. Bartolomeu flicked the switch on the wall next to the hidden entrance, opened the door, and stepped through.

A bare bulb illuminated a perfectly square chamber, no larger than eleven feet either way. The space had been lavishly furnished with the utmost care. Birds, stuffed and mounted on poles which were erected on elaborate wooden stands, lined the room in no particular order—an erudite looking crane, a pelican, a falcon with its wings outspread, a swan in beautiful repose. The walls behind them were paneled with smooth black wood from floor to waist and papered above with an elegant pattern in gold and dark crimson. Framed and mounted sculptures were placed upon the walls in auspicious positions, each one more curious than all the rest of them put together: a pair of ebony hands, one pierced by an arrow, the other holding an egg; an elephant sitting regally upon a gilded throne cast in resin; a wooden deer in a kimono blowing kisses to an unknown lover; a clock held upside-down with a protruding pendulum that had sprouted wings. In the center resided a modest stand, perhaps a simple altar, on top of which stood a tall white candle in a candlestick of emerald. Bartolomeu felt an indescribable resonance with the room. He could have remained within the space for days, yet he knew he mustn't.

Quickly, he headed back out. From the pantry he retrieved a book of matches and returned with them to the hidden chamber. He struck a match and lit the candle without a trace of ceremony or affectation. He closed the door, switched off the light, replaced the panel, and returned to the manor as if nothing out of the ordinary had taken place.

Somewhere in some distant heaven a light came on in a hidden house, attracting the attention of celestial dignitaries and their messengers. Registries were updated and sent to the proper authorities for the necessary approvals and notations. The requisite adjustments to angelic protocols were announced within the halls of the blessed. Affidavits woven from pure light were drafted, signed, notarized, inspected and filed, all with the efficiency and expertise befitting a holy institution.

Bartolomeu saw no reason to delay his departure. He knew he couldn't stay forever as an uninvited guest in an abandoned house. It had served its purpose, now it was time for him to move on. He knew not where he went, nor hardly cared. He would inevitably wind up someplace or another. He felt as if he were a man without a country, yet in no way unprepared to face the indignities of the day.

The world awaited, with bated breath, the culmination of the baptism of fire to which it had been subjected. Tensions grew on all sides. The consensus held that a conflagration of unendurable proportions was approaching. Unspeakable horrors would be suffered before the resulting mess was over. Whatever might be his role in the catastrophe to come, Bartolomeu harbored not a trace of doubt in his ability to play whatever part might be required of him, for he had placed himself, with full intent, into the house of service.

The Hour of the Minotaur

THE CARRIAGE was permeated with a fragrant haze of light blue smoke. Matthieu sat with his face next to the open window, the cool night air gently washing over his upper body as clusters of trees and open fields drenched in starlight passed by. The countryside revealed a luxurious indifference to the world which he was so happily leaving behind him. Stone houses lay sleeping in desolate meadows. The occasional square of pale orange light shone from a window without frame or glass. He imagined, knowing better, that the people who resided inside of them were aimless dilettantes and intellectuals, languishing in their freedom from the constraints of industry and accountability as if the entire countryside was an academic's impossible dream.

In the seat across from him sat a woman and her husband, he a stout bespectacled man dressed in the uniform of a minister of commerce, she a stone-faced matriarch graced with unambitious eyes of cruelty and disdain. They smoked their cigarettes in a semi-contemptuous silence, the man occasionally sparing a glance up at Matthieu as if to make a cursory offer of unspoken camaraderie while his wife gazed indolently through her faint reflection in the window. Matthieu had not a single thing to offer back to the man. He had exiled himself from the world to which they belonged, having divested himself of the yoke of his identity. He sought refuge from the company of others, not because the world had been unkind to him, but simply that he might familiarize himself, in peace and solitude, with something of the character of the man that he'd become.

If for no other reason than to further remove himself from the possibility of engagement with his fellow travelers, Matthieu slipped a hand into the leather satchel on the seat beside him and retrieved a thin and well-weathered booklet from its depths. The periodical was little more than a decade old. It comprised issue number four of the first volume of the hopelessly obscure *Knossos Journal*. The cover, front and back, was of impenetrable black, with title, date, and bylines printed in an austere font. On the front, below the title, appeared a depiction of a woman dressed in flowing robes with the head of a rat upon her delicate white shoulders. She ran, as if pursued, to the left side of the journal toward the spine, her bare arms reaching before her while her snout looked ever behind. Her one visible eye gleamed with a vivacity that at once suggested terror and delight. The back cover featured a single diminished image placed precisely in the center of the page, a woodcut print of an opened poppy flower, radiant in its magnificent solitude.

The journal was the latest of a handful of editions which Matthieu had painstakingly sought in recent months, each of which contained something of the written work of his late grandfather. He had yet to peruse the journal's pages. He'd been saving it for the train ride. Flipping to the front page, he scanned the table of contents. Between an article on the *Ungrund* of Jakob Boehme and an essay on abstract strategy games and ancient oracles lay his grandfather's piece, a short polemic bereft of title or description. He turned to the indicated page and submersed himself in the essence of the intoxicating prose.

Let my words appeal to the drunken, the sleeping, the abandoned, and the deranged; we who seek, yet must seek blindly; we who are forbidden to look upon the face of the beloved. Who among the chosen of us, anointed in our dreams by the blood of the Prophets, may locate the invisible Basilica beyond the veil of empire? Now is the time to rise up and shatter the very substance of the shadow of Leviathan. We who know the songs of exile must penetrate deep into the hidden source of Night, for here alone may the specters of monarchy, aristocracy, and democracy be allowed to consummate their ancient marriages with their long-maligned progenitors: tyranny, plutocracy, and anarchy. Here alone may we raise the banners of our secret ancestry, thus establishing the dominion of the sovereign whose name has long been lost to us.

The weak and small-minded hail the sun in its traversal through the heavens, never for an instant suspecting that they pay homage to a ghost, a phantom, a baseless illusion. The sky is clouded over by the wings of fallen angels. No more do they pursue the daughters

of men, those representatives of the enlightenment who have lost their luster, who are
forced to work in barren fields wielding plow-
shares and balance sheets, who bear the arms
of Erlbach and Corsica in their unthinking
obedience. The Watchers have renounced
their ancient lusts for the torchbearers of old
who have forsaken their torches. Their ardor
flames, upon the blackened altars of their
hearts, for the holders of the keys to which
no earthly lock is to be found. Whatever our
intentions, whatever our preferences, it cannot be denied that we shall be their stewards
in the world to come.

We must prepare ourselves, then. We
must refine our sensibilities. The fruit of our
transgressions must be forged into a vessel fit
to contain the sacred dew of heaven's pale fire.
A new era is upon us. Only those of us who
slake our thirst on waters ancient and forbidden may rise above the coming deluge.

Matthieu let the words wash over him, allowing himself
to absorb the prose as best he could. He made no attempt to
understand. He wished merely to taint his palate with the
flavor of the piece. After several minutes had passed, he put
the journal back into his satchel, avoiding any possibility of
eye contact with the couple who sat across from him.

The cigarette smoke which wafted in a continuous deluge toward his side of the cabin bothered him. He had peculiar sensitivities. Smoking was an activity to be indulged
in alone, he felt, particularly while engaged in intellectual

pursuits. If he smoked in the company of others, which was rare, it was only with the most trusted of confidants. He might share a cigarette with a lover, or with a friend of several years standing with whom he felt that it was possible to reveal something of his inmost nature. Smoking was an act of prayer, an accessory to the penetration of the veil of night, an intimate affair in which like-minded travelers might engage in an affront to the tyranny of day. To be subjected to the exhalations of a stranger was to tolerate a breach of ceremony approaching sacrilege.

When the couple finally disembarked, they left behind a memento, a small wooden box no larger than the palm of Matthieu's hand. He was so relieved to have rid himself of their company that he didn't notice the conspicuous item until the train had already pulled out of the station. Now, alone in the carriage, he took the curious relic in his hands. A black, silk ribbon protruded from beneath the lid of the box, allowing for its easy removal. Curious, he pulled the ribbon and removed the lid, placing it on the seat beside him. What lay beneath appeared to be a puzzle. Several blocks of flat, polished wood lay arranged in an asymmetrical arrangement. The blocks were of varying size and shape. They had characters printed on them, pictographic markings of iridescent gold which contrasted in a pleasing manner with the worn surfaces upon which they appeared. He couldn't quite identify the characters. They bore a vague resemblance to Chinese logograms, with which he harbored just enough familiarity to positively ascertain that these were something else.

He studied the arrangement of the blocks. He counted twenty-seven of them in total, with two empty spaces left open between them. A design appeared upon the lower surface, traced in delicate lines of lustrous silver visible only through the unoccupied spaces. Matthieu placed a finger on one of the characters. A gentle push was all it took to slide the piece into the space left open for it immediately below. The opening revealed another section of the design. He took another minute to examine the exquisite craftwork, then laid the ribbon back over the pieces and replaced the lid. Tracking down the owners in an attempt to return the item, he told himself, would be a futile undertaking. He unbuckled his satchel and deposited the item into a pocket of dark leather, relishing the solitude now afforded him as the train continued its sojourn through the night.

Matthieu took a taxi from the station. A single bag accompanied his satchel. His remaining possessions would arrive by post within the week. His needs were few. His suitcase contained two changes of clothes, a laptop, some books and notepads, a smattering of personal items. His new home was fully furnished, wired, and stocked with spirits of not inconsiderable quality. Though he'd never once laid eyes on it, he was affected by a curious sense of nostalgia, a sensation not unlike the uncanny familiarity afforded to the traveler in an unfamiliar place.

The house, a cottage really, had belonged to his grandfather on his father's side. For thirty-five years, the man had lived alone within its cherished walls. Matthieu's grandmother had fled by the time he'd moved in, gone to cavort around the world with an actor and drunkard of Russian descent. They scandalized the theater set while his grandfather remained in the shadows. He never sought to remarry, devoting the remainder of his years instead to his work, to the Lodge, to Virgil and Dante, to Milton and Blake.

Matthieu had never met the man. His mother had long harbored a nearly inhuman resentment for the other side of the family, with the result that one half of his heritage was shrouded in shadow. He'd scarcely known his father, and everything he knew about his grandfather had been learned from outside sources. Through some inscrutable accident of destiny he had inherited the house. A series of litiginous catastrophes had given way to unfathomable convolutions which, having taken on the momentum of a runaway train, could not be diverted to anyone's advantage but his own. Unfortunate events had taken place. Words had been uttered in haste. His mother would probably never speak to him again.

Relieved that his key did indeed fit the lock, Matthieu slipped in through the front door and switched on an over-head light. Thus was illuminated an ancient temple dedicated to the mysteries of toil and tradition. He set his bag down, closed the door behind him, and allowed himself to take in the illuminated study. The place was suffused with a particular character, a flavor of antiquity that promised to reveal lost myths and artifacts which lay buried in the rich, dark soil of his ancestry.

Enigmas foreshadowed by the writings of the man who'd lived there for so long were now laid bare before him. Upon an end table, below a column of maps pinned to the wall, stood a statue of a woman with a timepiece in her arms. Her body was swathed in flowing robes which, in all likelihood, had once been pristine, but were now stained black with dust and soot, among other unsavory substances. The hands of the clock appeared to have given up their weary ghost long before the man who'd placed it there had dropped his mortal shell. Elsewhere, a row of Piranesi prints framed in tarnished cedar crouched in the shadow of a stag's head above a rolltop desk. The faded ink, sepia inclined to foggy brown, depicted fragments of an empire lost to the imperious dominion of utility and expedience. Against the opposing wall, anchored like some unearthly colossus, sat a chipped and weathered writing desk of dark, heavy wood. An ivory horsehead table lamp, ancient and cracked, rose from one corner of the desk, white eyes gleaming with equine fire beneath the quiet auspices of the linen shade.

He imagined his grandfather sitting at the writing desk, bathed in the tawny glow of the lamp during the undignified hours of the night, applying himself with unbridled enthusiasm to laborious pursuits known to nobody but himself. There he would have studied canvas maps, complex technical diagrams, labyrinthine blueprints, and arcane charts. With drafting tools and inkwell he would plot the course of invisible forces through atmospheres so dignified that they defied the instruments of the more conventional sciences. On quieter nights, he'd let himself drown in thick volumes of prose or verse, tirelessly exploring works with which he'd long since attained an intimate familiarity.

His grandfather had purportedly been an obsessive man, devoted to long hours of work and study in fields which were hardly worthy of mention in polite society. It was known that he worked in naval intelligence, and that his work involved the processing of signals, the development of sonar and radar technologies, and the science of atmospherics. That he was a member of a Freemasonic order was no secret, though the particular Rite with which he had involved himself was kept concealed with a fastidiousness known only to those who have something to hide. His writings, few and scattered, were found between the covers of eclectic periodicals, technical journals, Freemasonic newsletters, and anthologies of the arcane. In the short space of seven months, Matthieu had managed to track down a formidable, if still incomplete, collection.

Ever since he was a child, he'd secretly harbored a fascination with his father's side of the family. When he had turned sixteen, his mother sat him down and calmly told him that his father had been dead for several years. His lineage, she said, with no uncertain disdain, had sprouted from a bad seed. She had done everything she could to strangle the vine of his father's blood within him, pruning the developing foliage wherever it threatened to come to fruition. She had married, he was made to understand, out of desperation, out of the folly of youth, as a direct result of deception and manipulation on his father's part—the story changed upon each telling, but the implication remained.

Matthieu had grown up very much his mother's son. He was fashioned with meticulous care in her image, yet the promise of forbidden fruit had never ceased to entice him. As he grew older, he began to make discreet inquiries, always kept hidden. Little by little, he'd gathered enough to fill a tiny dossier. In his twenty-eighth year, the dam had burst. By refusing to sell the house which he'd so unexpectedly inherited, he had severed the bond with his mother's lineage just as he'd re-established a connection with his father's. Now that he stood inside of his new home, he had no doubt that his crossing, as if from one side of a stream to the other, was irreversible.

Having savored something of the character of the front room, Matthieu lost no time in ensuring the accountability of the arrangements which he'd made for the house. His laptop was unpacked and laid upon the surface of the work desk with all of the respect and observance called for. Cables were attached, sockets plugged, connection to the outer world was confirmed. He had few other concerns. The faucets yielded a steady flow of water, drinkable or otherwise; the toilet flushed; most of the windows could be opened; he trusted that the icebox was in proper working order. He sent a quick email to the laboratory to affirm his availability.

He was dying to explore the house from top to bottom, but he forced himself to wait. Better to let himself ease gently into the spirit of the place, he thought, allowing it to suffuse his sensibilities in its own time. He'd had the foresight to bring along a bottle of Merlot, which he opened. He poured himself a glass, sat down in the wooden chair before the writing desk, removed the journal from his satchel, and perused the remainder of its contents. At length, torpor overtook him and he put himself to bed.

The following day was all but consumed with a steady stream of work: schematics to be uploaded, signal maps to be verified, route validations, test plans, and assessments to be meticulously carried out. Several hour's worth of phone calls, emails, and chat sessions allowed him no respite. At the end of the day, his livelihood duly secured, Matthieu closed the lid of his laptop and ceremoniously yanked out the cable. The pace of work would slow, he knew, as he settled into his new position. Over the course of many years, he'd watched the slow decline in responsibility awarded to those within the company who had reached the safe harbor of upper management. Within weeks his previous duties would pass to a team of fresh young engineers and his expertise would be utilized only as a resource. He would take his place as an oracle on demand and little more would be required of him. Early retirement, they called it unofficially. He could then be afforded the luxury of devoting the majority of his attention to matters of a far more personal interest.

The pleasure of his own undisturbed company mingled in an agreeable manner with the rich and desolate atmosphere of the house. He felt a million miles away from his co-workers. They took on the quality of abstractions. Already, he felt that he had become a different type of creature than he was before. He had transformed, as if by miracle, into a mystery which he himself had yet to solve.

Matthieu explored the remainder of the house as the last rays of the sun began to abandon their stations. It was by no means a large place. Aside from the main study and a bedroom, a kitchen and a little water closet, there remained only a modest basement. Down the stairs, around a corner, and through an unfinished doorway he went, emerging into an unexpectedly tasteful space with dark gray painted drywall and floors of sanded walnut. A heavy shelf lined one wall. A row of square receptacles hosted a collection of globes both earthly and celestial, along with tuning forks and pendulums, thick and dusty volumes, and stacks of paper bound with heavy black clips. A wrought iron wine rack extended from the floor to the ceiling next to a desk piled high with boxes. The bare bulb overhead, though not exactly opulent, provided a soft and unobtrusive glow which drenched the furnishings of the basement room in a soft patina of pale yellow light.

One particular shelf attracted his attention. Between two short stacks of musty books sat what looked to be some kind of radar or sonar device on top of a decorative cigar box. A circular screen of thick convex glass displayed the nebulous void of a cathode ray tube. Several knobs and dials were set into a copper display plate below. The whole was housed in a curved arch of stained wood of a style more often associated with radios and old clocks than with oscilloscopes and spectrum analyzers. Matthieu ran a finger across the sloping edge of the curious machine. It looked as if it belonged in a museum. He wondered if his grandfather had crafted it himself.

Several of the dials in the display were labeled with embossed tape. Many of these were peeling off as the adhesive substance beneath them had decayed with time and use. A quick glance at some of the labels aroused Matthieu's curiosity—"Onieric saturation levels," "Etheric Passage / Aion," "mimesis / diegesis"—the latter was found printed below a larger knob set just below the display tube and marked around the circumference with both positive and negative numbers. Matthieu wondered briefly if this was perhaps a sort of joke. It was just possible, he considered, that the curio was given to his grandfather as a gift by an associate with a perverse sense of humor.

A switch of unambiguous design sat nose-down to one side of the scope's metal panel. A cable ran from behind the small machine down to a monstrous box of sockets and outlets that protruded from the wall next to the floor. Matthieu pushed the switch into the "on" position and watched the convex screen as it expanded, without undue haste, into activity.

For the better part of a minute, nothing more exciting than a faint green glow occupied the screen. A momentary shudder disturbed the inactivity, followed by a series of rolling sweeps from right to left. The waves seemed to come at five-second intervals, always leaving in their wake a quickly fading trail of effervescent green light. Matthieu wondered if it mightn't be a test model intended only to verify the proper functioning of the display.

After watching the rolling wave for a space of several minutes, he noticed a tenuous form which persisted just an instant longer than the light trail. It was as if the fading signal clung to some invisible structure before losing its hold and dissolving back into the underlying sea of darkness. He began to play with some of the knobs in the hope of clarifying the form. Initially, the light was boosted so that the screen was nearly washed out, but a little experimentation allowed him to sharpen the display. There was no question about it—an opaque image, vaguely octagonal in shape, appeared on the right side of the display in the dissolving haze of each wave. Further messing about resulted in nothing new. He was intrigued, but could come to no conclusion. Intent on further investigation at a later date, he switched off the machine.

Back upstairs, his laptop closed and propped against one wall, he removed a thick binder from his suitcase along with a manageable portion of books. These he set upon the writing desk. He liked to devote his evenings to the compilation of his magnum opus. Picking up the tangled threads laid down by Giordano Bruno and John Dee, Ramon Lull and Francesco Giorgi, he sought to chart the course of angels through the invisible temple of Heaven's ancient and imperishable dominion. What began as a cursory inquiry, at most the makings of a brief article, had blossomed, over the course of several years, into a work of truly colossal proportions. His painstaking calculations had yielded a dense collection of diagrams and geometric studies, monstrous grids filled with letters and numbers, and page after page of notes and expositions detailing the ramifications of his research. He had charted the influence of angelic dignitaries with mathematical precision, detailed the unimaginable workings of the vast machinery of night, and plotted the secret harbors of the soul that the enterprising theurgist might better be equipped to storm the gates of heaven.

That his work might languish in obscurity he was well aware, his pursuits were of little interest to any but the specialist in a field few cared for or even knew of. He aspired to no more exalted a station than that of a reluctant footnote to the history of theology. His work, he felt, was worth doing for its own sake, whether a single soul other than his own was affected by it one way or the other. In truth, he harbored a perverse desire to disappear into his art. He would rub out his individual voice in an act of service to something incalculably larger than himself, finding refuge in a withdrawal from the world and all that it demanded of him. This, he considered, was the true delight of the scholar. It was at once a guilty pleasure and a continual act of prayer.

Several days and nights passed by in this manner, the early hours consumed with occupational responsibilities while the latter and more blessed hours were spent in the labor of his heart's true passion. When his calculations overwhelmed him, he would retrieve the wooden puzzle box. With the box on the surface of the desk before him, he would idle the minutes away, cigarette in hand, pushing the wooden blocks around to no discernible purpose.

The puzzle proved to be maddeningly unsolvable. He had not the slightest clue what the true objective of the game might be, or even if there was one. He simply wished to move the blocks around in such a way as to expose, little by little, the entirety of the image on the lower surface. He had uncovered the majority of the underlying design, enough to discern the form of a cathedral. Several areas around the edge had been difficult to expose, but with time and patience he had managed it. One of the larger pieces just below the center of the image remained nearly immovable. The piece obscured a sizable section of the upper façade of the cathedral, just below the base of a central peak. Matthieu might simply have removed the block from the enclosing box, thus revealing the concealed secret, but of course he wouldn't dare. Such an act would constitute so grave a heresy that he could never face his own reflection in the mirror again. The thought of shaving blindly for the remainder of his days prevented him from even considering the option, no matter how much the puzzle beguiled him.

As the weeks flowed by, Matthieu's duties lessened. The house became a place of familiarity to him, a sanctuary of labor and study, languor and seclusion. Its mysteries were swiftly becoming his own.

As his solitude approached perfection, he took to sipping vermouth in the evenings if the stars were properly aligned. A bookshelf stocked with atlases, historical studies, and manuals of cartography whispered formidable secrets to him as he drafted stratagems against the dictates of the reasonable world. He learned to listen to the slow creep of moonlight as its silver tide traced delicate indignities along the windowsills.

The block puzzle remained woefully unsolved. At length, he grew bored with the damn thing and left it to rot upon the rolltop desk. The basement offered a variety of suitable diversions by which to pacify his ravenous intellect in its stead. He found several documents of interest in the boxes stacked upon the desk. The letters were of particular interest to him, though of course they were nearly exclusively written not by his grandfather, but by the people with whom he maintained a correspondence. Poetry, art, literature, and history, along with some of the more obscure aspects of sonar technology were discussed at length. Often the letters were marked with what appeared to be Masonic insignia. Esoteric subjects were occasionally breached. Matthieu read through them slowly, no more than one or two per day, savoring their antiquated flavor and character. It would take him months to read them all.

A box of regalia was found in the bedroom closet: carefully folded robes, ceremonial swords, censers and chalices, along with several less comprehensible items. These, so he considered, were consecrated by hands other than his own. He was not inclined to disturb them.

He did, however, carry out a succession of experiments with the antiquated machine in the basement, each of which served only to confound him further. Turning on the power switch invariably produced the octagonal form on the display screen, yet it's location varied from time to time. Always it appeared within a certain radius. A series of readings at the top of every hour revealed a particular orbit in which it traveled. It completed its full course roughly once per day.

The cigar box which supported the machine, at first ignored, proved to be of interest upon further examination. No brand or slogan tarnished the purity of the thing. The lid displayed an image of a house of worship beneath a radiant bell tower clothed in the intimate embrace of starlight. The form of the church, Matthieu noted, bore a vague resemblance to the image on the bottom of the block puzzle. Indeed, a circular window appeared beneath the tower in precisely the section of the building where, were it swapped with the image on the puzzle, it would be obscured by the immovable block.

Inside the box was found a small collection of what appeared to be war medals. From where they might have come, or from what era they hailed, Matthieu couldn't say. The ribbons were dominated by bold shades of red, black, green, and white, while the medals themselves shone with the dull luster of tarnished bronze and copper. Winged eagles, blazing stars, brazen oxen, and winding serpents appeared above crosses, polygons, and other geometrical forms. To the last of them, they were engraved with names: 'Azazel', 'Kokab', 'Penemue', 'Saraiel', along with several others.

Matthieu took one of the medals in his hand, a Maltese cross which hung from a ribbon of white and red. A circle of brass in the center revealed an embossed image of a man in robes upon the peak of a hill or mountain. An upturned crescent below displayed the title 'Arkas'. He passed a thumb over the raised image, savoring the weight of the metal on his outstretched fingers before putting it back into the box.

Along with the medallions were found several items of no uncertain interest. Below the metallic emblems, folded over three times, lay a rough cloth of white muslin. When unfolded, the fabric revealed six white cigarettes lying side by side like elongated doves. He took the edges of the sheet between his fingers and lifted it to his nose. The rich tobacco was still infused with a freshness rarely found in packaged cigarettes. He carefully wrapped the treasure up again and replaced the cloth. On the other side of the box was found a small notebook bound in deteriorated red leather. Lastly, taped to the underside of the lid, was a tiny compass.

The notebook, he suspected, would require a more thorough examination than he wished to invest in it at the moment. He took it out of the box and placed in on the shelf. Beneath it lay an old photograph of a man in a cap and blue-gray greatcoat. The insignia on his collar were impossible to make out in the murky half-tone of the photographic print. The man's right eye was entirely covered by bandages. His was not the face of Matthieu's grandfather, but there were enough similarities to mark him as a not so distant ancestor. The stoic lines below the cheekbones, the humorless jaw, and the weary brow were not dissimilar to those of his father's. He flipped the photograph over to find a single phrase written in dark blue ink: 'The wounded sentry stationed at the heart of desolation's empire.'

He put the photograph aside and pulled the compass free from the inner surface of the lid. A close inspection of the device revealed a curious quality. The red end of the needle, no matter how he rotated the compass, remained fixed upon a point which lay significantly shy of magnetic north. Thinking perhaps that the basement room was oriented at a tilt, he took the device upstairs to check the bearings by the northern star. Even given the natural degree of difference between magnetic north and true north, the needle remained steadfast in its errant position. Perplexed, he simply put it back into the box, the tape still dangling by one end from the underside of the lid.

Later, having spent a considerable amount of time at work on his ever-evolving thesis, he sat out on the back porch with a cigarette and perused the contents of the notebook by the pale light of the overhead lamp. The book appeared to be a journal of sorts. The entries were few and written in pencil by a somewhat shaky hand.

Matthieu flipped idly through the blank pages in the latter half of the journal. All of them were empty except for a page near the end which had been marked up in different handwriting than that of the earlier sections. A pen and ink sketch of a man with the massive head of a bull dominated the page. He was dressed in ceremonial robes which fell in swathes around his body. One uplifted hand raised a scepter into the air above him. Seven stars, skillfully depicted, stood lined up in a row above his large, protruding horns. Above them was written, in an elegant script, *Alkaid—above the celestial Virgin in the North—chicory with wormwood, magnetic lodestone*.

Matthieu recognized the correspondences. Alkaid was the outermost star in the tail of the Great Bear, chief among the constellations which revolve around the pole star in the center of the northern sky. Alkaid was identified in Agrippa's books of occult philosophy as one of fifteen stars said to be possessed of potent magical qualities. The attributions of chicory, wormwood, magnetic lodestone, and the bull were all listed there, having been derived from earlier sources whose origins lay in obscurity.

Turning back to the journal entries at the beginning of the book, Matthieu read through the text in a single sitting.

❂

November 4, 1918. *The Hour of the Wolf*

My broken body lies beneath an artificial sun replete with shining crystals in a sky composed of panels of black painted wood. I write with my left hand, the bones in my right hand have been shattered. Several ribs are cracked. It hurts to breathe. Of all of my infirmities, my eyes have proven by far the most bothersome. My right eye throbs and itches like the mark of Cain beneath the bandages. I don't dare scratch it, lest I injure myself further. My other eye, the operative oculus, is now painfully sensitive to sunlight. I can barely make out my own miserable scrawl.

At my gentle, yet persistent, requests, they've finally moved me from the common area into a secluded enclosure. Large portraits set within heavy golden frames hang against the soft black painted walls of this compact little room. Countenances regal and majestic are rendered in delicate brushwork upon their surfaces. They shine above stout bodies in fine uniforms decorated with ancient and unintelligible insignia. I have tried in vain to locate the precise point at which their noble gazes converge. I have convinced myself that it's a geometrical impossibility, though in all likelihood it's simply a testament to my diminished eyesight.

I am a ghost, a casualty of strategy; I've grown so slight I fear I'll slip into the cracks between the bandages. I haven't the slightest clue as to where I am. The doctor merely grunts in response to my questions. The nurses, like stoic sphinxes, respond with questions of their own. At other times they offer admonitions. I ought to turn all of my thoughts toward a successful recovery, they tell me. I understand, from observation, that I'm in a private residence which has been converted into a hospital. I don't think that my wounds are so serious, but to be perfectly honest I don't particularly care one way or the other.

My father, with the weight of his ancestry behind him, often after consuming a quantity of vermouth, is quite fond of waxing eloquent about a place which he identifies only as The Basilica. This is the very chapel written of in the ancient Book of Splendor, so he claims, in which the fallen world is reconciled with its source in the eternal. The affectation is not unique to him. I come from a long line of dissidents and poets. Our blood is tainted with fanciful ideas. Alas, I am similarly affected. I expect I must make for an unprofitable soldier.

Before the blast had relieved me of my senses, I may have caught a glimpse of the elusive edifice. Now it affects me like a disease. I can think of little else. My inheritance has come to claim me at this most opportune of times. I lie entirely unoccupied in this dusty little antechamber, surrounded by the distant groans and wailings of those who suffer more than I do. There is little else for me to do but apply myself diligently to the penetration of night's inner sanctum. I would look once more upon the face of the eternal.

With the determination afforded to the ruined, I turn my vision inward. Sumptuous landscapes appear in the reflective surface of my convalescence. Phantoms half-formed and scarcely understood taunt me with un-intelligible shadow-plays. They assume the faces of my fallen comrades. They carry on in a manner at once portentous and obscene atop crumbling porticoes and monstrous archways bathed in moonlight. Abandoning their insidious pantomimes, I turn to wander through a labyrinth of war-torn city streets thick with fog and mist, searching for traces of the thread which I have dropped so many times. I would follow its perambulations down winding avenues and alleyways, along the corridors of memory, deep into the uncharted hours of the night.

Like steel, I'm tempered by successive periods of sleep and wakefulness. I sleep beneath a dazzling chandelier which hangs suspended from the ceiling above me; I wake to the pale white fire of interior stars. The utterances of ancient oracles are fused with the mindless slogans of the vulgar in the fires of this visionary forge. I can hardly hope to offer anything worthy of the dignity of my ambition. What little eloquence I have left to me is to my detriment. My words create a debt that I cannot repay. They issue forth like the last pitiable cry of a forgotten aristocracy, swallowed up by vicious winds beneath the limpid starlight.

I have been ceremonially stripped of all titles, honors, dignities. My expulsion from the fraternal order of the trenches is my one remaining virtue. The anxiety of my exile is transmuted, in the alembic of my wounded body, into a potent dew with which to redeem the sins of my progenitors. By these means, I seek a purity which exceeds that of my station and duties in the daylight world. Thus, perhaps, may I be granted an audience with the undying.

I am well aware of the dangers inherent in my internal wandering, my search for the perfection which I beheld in the light which took my eye from me. The truly pure never last. He who stands without taint is fit only to be devoured by wolves. I am not afraid to face my fate. I only wish that I could be devoured all the sooner. Only when I have been reduced to nothing, or very nearly so, might I be made light enough to pass beyond the winds which veil the very heart of night.

In my vanity, I flatter myself that I resemble Wotan with my injured eye. It is prophesied, in the Icelandic Gylfaginning, that the wolf Fenrir will consume the one-eyed god. This only after the sun and moon and shining stars have been devoured by the sons of the wolf. Fenrir, in his turn, will be killed by Wotan's son in an act of vengeance. But I am not the same as he. If I carry out my tasks correctly, there will scarcely be anything left to avenge.

November 6, 1918. *The Hour of the Silence*

I have penetrated into the hour of silence, not so difficult a task as one would imagine. One thousand chattering voices have besieged me, and yet I've managed to drown them, one after another.

The pain, the throbbing, the itching, they are as fires doused by the rolling tide of darkness. Howling winds enwrap the ensuing silence like an endless roll of gauze. They uplift me, these winds, my nature is exalted by them rather than dispersed. I arise like a speck of illuminated dust into a courtyard filled with weeping angels.

Here, in this nocturnal country, the mourners howl and wail for the living. Their miserable lamentations flow like rivulets down streets of onyx. I strive against the currents. I must escape from their infernal racket. Quite by accident, I come to the source of the overflowing waters, the cause of all the fits and tantrums indulged in by these ministers of melancholy. Here, beyond the tumultuous outpouring, I find at last the gate that I've been searching for. Having not an ounce of caution or discretion, I slip through like a thief.

November 6, 1918. *The Hour of Lead*

Back in my little bed, I'm again made subject to the penetrating gaze of my accusers, the unnamed officers who occupy the portraits on the walls around me. I can only see a handful of them. The radius of my gaze is limited by the constraints imposed upon my body. I can't turn my head more than a little to either side, nor can I crane my neck back far enough to see behind me. There's a mirror sitting upon a ledge on the far wall, but, due to its angle and to mine, it reflects only a section of the ceiling.

My sight is further hampered by a constant dusk, an infernal mist which enwraps and obscures my surroundings and limits my peripheral vision. My wounded eye ever announces its presence with a steady pulse of pain. I can see it in my mind's eye, the only reliable instrument left to me. It appears as a dismal, burnt-out orb mired in a casement of murky tar.

I am seldom left alone for long enough to make serious progress in my search. The nurses come at regular intervals to pester and disturb my meditations. They indulge in idle gossip while they change the bandages. The injections threaten to disperse my concentrated efforts like doves before a hail of gunfire. The sheaths of silence crack and break beneath the strain. I drift into a nostalgic malaise, unable again to locate the suture in the veil which renders the night opaque.

When I was young I used to spend innumerable hours in my father's study gazing at old photographs. Among the images of my antecedents, and the surviving works and journals of their predecessors, I found a hidden thread by which I might unwind necessity itself. Thus was born an unspoken agenda which I've carried with me ever since. This thread has led me along a perilous route through the halls of academia and apprenticeship, into the dismal embrace of a loveless marriage, through insidious canals lined with heavy artillery intent on reducing the last bastions of order and civilization to smoke and rubble. Whatever the cost, however calamitous my destiny, I will follow it to the very end. It will lead me, I have no doubt, to the Basilica itself.

I have done unpardonable things in my pursuit. I've added to the transgressions of my parents and bound myself all the more to the errors of my lineage. The world is a vast and unintelligible beast. Conspiracies of nature and industry lead us through an absurd pantomime of somnambulistic gestures. We play the roles allotted to us in a mockery of destiny beneath a blind and autocratic sun. Our performances are inevitably 'solitary, poor, nasty, brutish, and short.' The state has proven incapable of redeeming the iniquities of nature. The empire of the rational has failed us. Our diplomats have led us to the trenches beneath the unceasing roar of black abominations. Our last hope lies in abandonment: of ourselves, of our conventions, of all our names and images. Taking leave of our senses, we must surrender to the very pivot of heaven, never ceasing our struggle until we've stormed the final gate and overthrown the monarch on the threshold.

I will again attempt to pick up the threads of my pursuit tomorrow. For now, it's all that I can do to simply sink into the soft embrace of sleep, wondering as I drift into the darkness which of heaven's rebellious angels first instructed us in the forbidden arts of trench warfare, of wireless telegraphy, of depth charges and strategic bombing raids.

November 7, 1918. *The Hour of the Minotaur*

An officer has come to speak with me. His speech is nearly incoherent. He asks me questions and I answer them as best I can. I note a look of concern upon his face. I suppose I ramble, or speak of things I ought not to. To hell with them. Let them lock me up if they feel the need. I don't care.

To be fair, I must concede that I am not a reasonable man. Flights of near delirium consume me for hours at a time. In my hallucinatory fervor, I sometimes fall prey to the delusion that the august faces who appear in the portraits before me are those of my own ancestors. I fancy that I recognize traces of my features in their stern regards. Their uniforms would seem to reveal all the secret glories concealed in my blood. Those stolid tableaux composed of epaulets and shining medals, honorary sashes and rows of polished buttons transform, in my fevered mind, into variations on a coat of arms in which are encoded the traditions of my lineage. I'm sometimes startled by the sound of my own voice, muttering incoherent questions in hopes of receiving some form of guidance from these misbegotten prophets.

When lucidity is restored to me I return to the empire of night, far from the doctors and the officers. I follow my tattered thread through the gaps within my memory and into the forbidden places. Here, I behold the husks of venerable saints consumed by sacerdotal fires long since extinguished. Their blackened hands clutch pale yellow parchments bearing the titles of their offices and dignities. Upon them may be found the addresses of administrative mansions concealed by the radiance of starlight, the domiciles of greatly honored clerks of conscience and remorse, those esteemed executives of the archives and indexes of Heaven.

I let myself rise further into the heart of the sublime, passing through holy palaces of Kabbalistic splendor. There, the shining hearts of night's pale luminaries lie unprotected on unpainted, wooden tables. Their names have been forgotten, their attributions rubbed out of all the manuals of art and science. One after another, I trespass their inner sanctuaries. A veil is rent, a vessel shattered, the shadow of the minotaur lies petrified before the flame which rises from the presiding altar. It is essential that I remain undetected lest all these shadows solidify into a single terrifying revelation.

I emerge again into a city besieged by the memory of atrocity. Images imprinted upon the silver nitrate of my soul replay themselves in subtle shades and variations. Sirens wail at the approach of incoming aircraft under cracked and blackened skies. The denizens of the nighttime city stalk the streets in a somnambulistic daze. They have been ushered from their homes with great solemnity. They've had no time to prepare themselves for the conflagration which has thus befallen them.

A troop of shell-shocked carabiniers drifts by, border guards from a country erased from history, too stunned by the revelations of sunset to acknowledge my pleas for some indication of their point of origin. Detonations sunder brick from window frame. Flashing lights devour the sky amidst the roar and thunder of annihilating angels. I spot the shadow of The Basilica in the distance in the light of a tumultuous explosion, but I'm disoriented, and the stars are obscured by thick gray smoke.

I wander blindly in the aftermath of the attack. I've paced these winding streets a thousand times, but always the crucial junction eludes me. The center of this labyrinth is inaccessible by its very nature. It stands unguarded. There is no danger. Yet only the fallen may find it. Would that I could simply pitch myself from atop the perilous cliffs, dashing my wounded body onto the rocks below, but alas, I've reduced myself so much that I've grown lighter than the air itself. Always, the winds bear me upward.

November 8, 1918. *The Hour of Pitch*

The doctor informs me that my wounds are healing as expected. I remain compliant, content to follow orders to the very end. The chandelier seems to rock and sway above me like a tiny vessel on wind-swept waves. The voices continue, but I scarcely hear them. They've set me further upright in my bed. My view of the room has been dramatically altered. My gaze is now fixed upon the mantelpiece.

There, between four black urns topped with silver, before a mirror framed in elaborate gold leaf, stands a modest statue of a woman with skin as black as pitch. One arm is wrapped around a tall white candle which rises from a vase. Her countenance is of a radiant darkness attributed to the sons of Heaven. I cannot doubt that it is an image fashioned in the likeness of She, the Goddess Night, the Queen of the Canticles.

Beyond the backside of the woman, reflected in the mirror, hanging before the wall behind my head, I can just make out the reflection of an ornamental brass lamp. From one end of the lamp, beneath the body of a peacock with elaborate tail feathers, arises a lambent flame, its light nearly choked in the thick air and the droning voices of the doctor and his aides. There are no portraits on this back wall, merely a wide expanse of flat black paint adorned with traceries of gold. Ghostly forms compose themselves in the flickering incandescence of the light; an unfolding tapestry of horse hooves, desert landscapes, rolling fog. The pale reflection of the flame, heightened by the play of light upon the surface of the mirror, makes the wall behind me appear vaguely translucent, as if it were the shimmering surface of a veil.

Left alone again, I find my way back into the intolerable darkness. I bathe myself in the most impenetrable hour of the night, for it is night that heals me of my wounds, not time nor medicine. The last of the stellar lights have now been swallowed by the sons of the wolf. The stars no longer shine, nor moon nor sun nor anything at all. In the ensuing darkness, I can just make out the faint lights of the city which lies across the vastness of the waters, that ocean of blood and influence which separates me from my distant ancestry.

I must push on. I yearn for an oblivion which I cannot attain. Forgetfulness will not be granted. The night will not allow it of me. Having reached the center of the labyrinth and faced the axis of my destiny, the route must remain engraved in memory for generations to come.

Carried unceasingly now on the currents of twilight's untarnished splendor, I approach

the opposing shores under cover of an unbearable silence. By routes unnavigable and
obscure have I come to the end of the line.
Here, in that magnificent city lost to history, I alone, having reduced myself to nearly
nothing, may steal into the court of heaven's
monarchy and snuff out the very source of
light.

November 8, 1918. *The Hour of Destiny*

The empire of day has crumbled. Dusk
has stained the last horizon. Under cover of
eternal night I now might enter The Basilica
unseen, there to find the poison which has
so gloriously tainted my bloodline. Like
Wotan, I will fill my mouth with night's black
ichor, the vitriolic dew of stars infernal and
insatiable, thence to ferry the intoxicating
liqueur back to the waking world. There will
it be released as an offering to the poetic soul,
a body glorified, a shining beacon whose light
will set the world afire.

November 11, 1918. *The Hour of Sapphire*

I have arrived at The Basilica at last.
Beyond this, no more may be spoken.

Matthieu adopted the journal as a talisman of sorts over the weeks to follow. By day it lay concealed atop the cigar box in the basement, only to be retrieved at night and propped up against the horsehead lamp, thus to shed a subtle influence over the charts and graphs, the expositions and the exegesis, those nightly distillations of midnight's insoluble oil.

He quietly exulted in the legacy left to him through his father's bloodline. He felt as if he'd discovered a rich vein of precious metal lying deep within a concealed place. His findings were perplexing, to be sure, yet he felt a certain resonance with the wounded soldier's account. His hope was that his own work might retain an impression of the revelations found within the journal, affected through a combination of proximity, sympathy, and heritage. The thought that he might himself pick up the thread laid down within its pages pleased him.

No less than a week after he'd first laid eyes on it, Matthieu suffered an epiphany regarding the compass which he'd found taped to the lid of the cigar box. He'd been walking along the meager trickle of a creek which passed through the outer edge of the property, gazing wistfully at what little starlight could be seen on such an overcast night. Polaris glared benevolently from the north, while the tail of the great bear was just visible through a break in the cloud. A gentle revelation was bestowed upon him from the auspices of the terminal star. Without hesitation, he headed for the basement.

The thought which had so taken him was whimsical and absurd, he knew. He had no illusion as to the plausibility of the notion. And yet, driven by an irrational impulse which he had no desire to deny himself, he retrieved the compass, took it back outdoors, and checked the position of the needle against the starry night sky. He was somewhat shocked to find that his suspicion was confirmed: the needle, still errant of true north, yet by a different degree than before, pointed directly toward the star Alkaid.

How, he thought, could such a thing be possible? He'd assumed, when he first laid eyes on it, that some foreign element had perhaps contaminated the magnetic bar. It would never have occurred to him that the position of the needle might vary over time. Having determined the nature of the irregularity, a few hour's wait provided him with ample evidence that the indicator of the compass was indeed fixed upon the propitious star. It vacillated with the motion of the heavenly dignitary, following it around the milky void as it disappeared and again emerged from cover of cloud. It followed that twice per day, depending on the time of year, the two norths would converge for a brief period.

Having ascertained the nature, if not quite the purpose, of the compass, he turned his thoughts to the machine he'd found sitting atop the cigar box. It seemed just plausible to him that the signal which vacillated from place to place on the convex display might be similarly oriented. Less than an hour's observation was enough to determine the route along which the signal passed. It would seem to move in an orbit roughly opposing that of the minotaur's star. It pulsed and flickered as it meandered along its course, growing and diminishing in strength. Matthieu couldn't help but regard it as a reflected image of the star, endlessly circumnavigating the center of its labyrinth. But where, he wondered, might the entrance to that labyrinth be found?

146

Matthieu's fingertips ran along the character embossed into the central block within the wooden puzzle. It lay upon the writing desk among several stacks of paper. He was no longer concerned with the displacement of the central piece. He had lost all interest in "solving" the enigma. The device had ceased to function as a game for him. Rather, like the journal, it had taken on the significance of a fetish.

The Basilica called out to him with a subtle, yet persistent voice, a gentle pull from the nether regions of the soul. It was futile to resist the summons. His very blood was bound to it like a hammer to its anvil, or the rose unto the cross. In one way or another, he would find a key to night's concealed empire. Thus he would abscond from the waking world only to reappear within the winding streets and byways of the nocturnal city first uncovered by his ancestor.

He had no shortage of possible methods of ingress. He'd studied far and wide, he was familiar with a thousand ceremonial techniques which had been used throughout the ages, yet he felt that it was necessary to improvise. A rite that had been written by another hand, or which had been previously performed so much as a single time, would simply not be suitable. The route must be unique to him, he felt. The path must be untrodden. As he idly toyed with the sliding blocks, manipulating them to no discernable purpose, the outline of a rite began to formulate within him.

In the bedroom, atop a short white dresser opposite the somewhat spartan bed, stood an elaborately framed mirror large enough to reflect the entirety of his body, so long as he was seated. Grasping the unwieldy beast between his outstretched arms, he transported it down the narrow stairway to the basement, taking great care to avoid scuffing the frame as he navigated the corner halfway down. The mirror was set down in the south, resting upright against the wine rack.

He removed the compass from its box and checked the needle. In five hour's time, according to a quick mental calculation, the star Alkaid would appear directly above, or behind, the pole star in the center of the heavens. To the naked eye, it would appear as if the fateful star was north of the northernmost point of the celestial sphere, inhabiting an unmappable region beyond the confines of the compass. Whatever it was that was indicated by the signal on the oscilloscope, according to Matthieu's fanciful logic, ought then to be accessible through a suitable gateway in the south.

Preparations for departure were duly made. The cigarettes were taken from their enfolding cloth in the cigar box and laid out in a row before the mirror. The first of them he painted, just above the base, with a tiny pictographic symbol traditionally attributed to Alkaid. The fourth he similarly marked with the character that appeared on the central piece of the sliding block puzzle. The puzzle itself, with its center still concealed, was placed to one side in full view of the mirror. The photograph of the man with the bandage around his eye was also set before the glass, along with the war medals and the journal. Candles were placed to either side, their flames lying outside of the range of reflection. The compass was placed upright just behind the mirror. Four hours remained before the star converged with true magnetic north. A cigarette would mark the beginning of each hour. Two cigarettes would then remain for the hours beyond the veil of night.

Matthieu set himself down before the mirror, taking care to ensure that he was comfortable enough to sit in one position for some time to come. A matchbox sat within reach upon the cigar box, which stood propped against the bookshelf to one side. The box was opened, a match retrieved, the phosphorous ignited and the first of the cigarettes was lit.

The tobacco was far more pungent than Matthieu had expected. It retained a hint of its former glory, a trace of rich aroma clung to the acrid smoke like a dying ghost. Matthieu exhaled the first lungful against the mirror's surface, consecrating it for ceremonial use. He set the remainder of the cigarette down upon a small white dish, allowing what remaining smoke it had to offer to rise like incense and fumigate the temple with its dark, astringent fog. Thus, amidst an aromatic haze, began *The Hour of the Wolf.*

Matthieu kept his gaze firmly fixed upon his reflection. The optical effects began almost immediately. Pools of shadow and discoloration morphed and shifted across the contours of his face, giving rise to a host of phantasmal forms. The space around the eyes was particularly affected. All but the slightest vestiges of peripheral vision were entirely lost in the surrounding morass. He kept his body poised and his breath carefully measured. The minutes crept by as if through thick molasses.

After a tedious hour had passed with little incident, the sound of a bell, electronically synthesized by his cell phone, rang resonant throughout the room. The second cigarette was initiated in silence, his gaze held still, his body perfectly inflexible.

The hour to follow gave way to a new class of optical phenomena. The defining characteristics of Matthieu's face took on an uncanny unfamiliarity. It was as if he'd never looked upon his own reflection before. The features of the image had not changed overmuch, they were simply no longer recognizable as his own. His surroundings had by now been entirely submerged into a perceptual fog. His torso appeared to him as little more than an indistinguishable blur. Gradually, and with great subtlety, he came to recognize his father's sardonic eyes on the other side of the glass. His grandfather, as well, appeared before him, followed by the stoic and regal bearing of the wounded soldier. In the obscurity of his peripheral vision, he could almost make out traces of a military uniform. Within minutes, even this had given way to a tapestry of bandages and gauze.

Matthieu continued to follow the thread as the hour stretched on, passing ever deeper into the strata of his heritage. A gallery of portentous apparitions paraded their soft enigmas in the glass. They peered at him with scrutinizing glances, those half-familiar ciphers of flesh and expression, each upholding the tenets of a tradition passed in silence through the blood of successive generations. He gazed upon the testaments of the wretched and the noble, the timorous and the bold. Again the alarm sounded, breaking the silence of his waking dream. Another cigarette was ignited in the flickering half-light of the candle flames. By the time it had been left to smolder on the dish, the reflection in the mirror had changed once again.

Matthieu looked now upon a countenance bereft of qualities, a face of emptiness, an expressionless mask having not a single trait or affectation. Just as Polaris, the Watcher of the North, having no longitudinal degree, partakes at once of the nature of every star and of none, so did this visage contain the nature of the entirety of the bloodline. He had no doubt that he'd reached the guardian of the threshold, the master of the veil, the patrilinear watcher at the border of inscrutable night. Sharing no secrets, betraying no revelation, the monotony of the sentinel's gaze was nearly unbearable. The entirety of the hour passed without a single reprieve from the interrogating glare. The soft ring of the alarm bell, when it finally occurred, was as a blessing from the highest heaven. He knew that he had successfully penetrated the outermost veil. *The Hour of the Minotaur* now lay before him.

He was scarcely aware of the process of lighting the fourth cigarette, so completely had he slipped into the depths of visionary trance. His body was lost to sensation, his surroundings were subsumed by starlight, he could no longer discern whether his eyes remained open or whether they had closed. He trusted that the remaining cigarettes could take care of themselves and allowed himself to slip into the luminous void. Like a mote of dust on rolling waves of tar, he was flung without leave across the gulf of the firmament and into the city of perilous night.

Beneath monstrous towers and abandoned parapets he searched for absolution in that terrible place. His way was lit by flaming torches upheld by ancient hands. The sons of seraphim cast down from paradise wandered the dusk-stained city streets. Their devastating flames shone forth like beacons from crumbling balconies and ruined terraces. Rivers of milk and ectoplasm flowed freely beneath the subterranean stars, flooding the gutters and threatening to sweep the unwary into their ravenous currents. Matthieu passed by the daughters of Anaeas, their howls and lamentations echoing from the blasted domes of scattered rotundas. Still, they searched for the Cumean sibyl whose revelations had so long ago enflamed their sire.

He passed through a series of high and desolate mansions arranged in ever-expanding concentric tiers. Here, before the dolorous gaze of the murderers of Albion, he received a missive from an emissary of an office in the Basilica. He arrived at a chapel besieged by Nephilim; its steeple lost in mist and fog, its foundations decayed by apostasy. The angel Semyaza, leader of the rebellious hosts, awaited him inside the sacristy, barricaded there so as to spare his legions the devastating fire of his countenance. Matthieu stood outside the sacristy door as the murmurings of unwashed Cherubim bathed his weary limbs and reverent brow. After what seemed like an eternity of waiting, an unambiguous order was issued through the heavy wooden barricade. He was ceremonially bound to a covenant long since established by the blood of his progenitors. The terms of his service eclipsed his name, his self-image, all his personal agendas: he was to sever the bond between faith and doctrine, to overthrow the tyranny of necessity, to reestablish the ascendancy of Mystery in the Temple of the Uttermost Night.

Assailed by neither doubt nor conscience, failure having lost its meaning in the wake of his transgressions, he set out to fulfill the demands of his inheritance. He had nothing left to lose, no life to go back to, no regrets to atone for. The Basilica awaited him and he had not a shadow of a doubt that he would reach it by subtlety or by force.

The Star of Gnosia

MARINO was the oldest, but so impetuous was Estrela that the others let her take the lead. Roughly half of the passages that appeared in the rite were too insipid for her taste, so they set about penning elaborations of their own. In addition to countless alterations and amendments, they'd managed to craft a constitution. They would henceforth be known among themselves as 'The Holy Order of the Star of Gnosia'.

Silvestre had come up with the elaborate name, having found the title in a book on stellar navigation. *Gnosia* referred to the brightest of the stars in the constellation of the Northern Crown. He'd initially assumed that this was a reference to the Gnostics, before Marino, ever the young scholar, pointed out that it was in fact a Latinized form of Knossos, the oldest city in all of Europe. This so appealed to the three of them that the name became official.

The rite itself was taken from the pages of a hand-bound book found in their father's private library. The author, a Frater L.I.L., wrote in a turgid, self-important prose that the trio alternately mocked and imitated in their founding document. The majority of the book concerned itself with such tedious topics as the ethics and conduct of an initiate, the roots of the work in the traditions of antiquity, and the dietary restrictions to be observed on certain holy days. The devotional ceremony in the latter section alone captured their imagination. A handful of additional volumes found in the small library likewise attracted their interest. Much of the collection was written in French, which, while it could generally be understood, constituted too much of an effort to bother with.

Marino retrieved a tattered volume on the Kabbalists of Castile, the cover of which had nearly come clean off. Estrela was attracted to a fine translation of Francis Barrett's massive tome, *The Magus*, with its elaborate tables, correspondences, lists of spirits, and orations. Silvestre, for his part, refused to settle on a single book to study, preferring instead to sample the contents of several books at once. They renounced their classes and their chores that they might apply themselves with perfect assiduity to their new curriculum. They knew that they would have to work without undue distraction. Within the space of two short weeks they must become as living gods.

They were thankful for what little time they had. Initially, they'd planned to spend the duration of the weekend merely inspecting the forbidden library, along with anything else of interest that might be found inside the upstairs office. The door had been secured before their father had left the house, but such a simple lock hardly proved a match for Silvestre's skilled hand. The letter arrived on Saturday, the sixteenth day of April, by which point they'd evaluated every volume on the shelf.

The brief note read as follows:

Silvestre, Estrela, Marino,

My intention was to leave you in charge of the house for a period of no more than three days. As it happens, my return will be delayed. I've run into some trouble in Seville, details to follow on my return. I will be gone for no less than fifteen days. Please seek the assistance of your uncle Bonifacio (this was their late mother's brother, whom they had no intention of contacting), he will tend to matters of the house and prepare your meals. If he makes noises in regard to the bother, you must simply remind him of the tremendous debt that he owes to the family. There will be no need to explain. He will understand and acquiesce.

My thoughts and prayers are with you as always,

Esteban

The lock on the office door had again to be picked, as Silvestre had already re-secured it from the other side and absconded through an office window. By the time the sun had reached the western horizon, they'd come to the unanimous decision to undertake a concentrated period of spiritual work. Their goal, as recorded in their constitution, was the attainment of gnostic awakening, the highest degree of apotheosis, and the realization of the Star of Gnosia within the chapel of their inmost hearts. "We'll steal the fire from a heaven which is forbidden to us and turn it toward the exaltation of our souls," maintained Estrela. "Any other application would constitute an act of heresy."

They were to begin the work with the initial rite they'd taken from the book. By the time the sun had again risen in the east, this had been transformed into an invocation of their own devising. During the hours following sunset on Sunday, the 17th of April, they would each perform the rite in turn, two of them acting as facilitators while one performed the incantations. Silvestre, being the youngest, would go first, then Estrela and Marino. The rite would be followed by several hours of silent devotion, each in separate rooms within the house. This would be maintained until the urge for sleep so overwhelmed them that they could remain awake no longer.

By the time the rites began, the trio had already fallen subject to a mild state of delirium. None of them had managed to sleep for more than an hour at a time since the official commencement of their Order. They performed their long devotions in the manor's basement, among a cumbersome labyrinth of old and long-neglected furniture. A curtain of black velvet was hung in the north from tiny hooks screwed into the beams that ran along the ceiling. Two standing candelabras that had not seen the light of day for several years were set before the obsidian backdrop. The flicker of the flames cast a mesmeric dance of shadows throughout the secluded space, heightening the narcotic effect of their sonorous recitations.

The first of the ceremonies passed without a single complication. Silvestre's delivery, though somewhat stilted, was genuinely heartfelt. The reverberation of his voice inspired a potent flame of aspiration in his siblings, both of whom felt that the space was effectively sanctified by his efforts. The emanations called forth by his rhythmic entreaty seemed to rise up through the floorboards and ennoble even the remotest chambers of their domicile. A sublime quietude descended upon the basement in the wake of the bell's final strike, fortifying the hearts of all three participants for the trials to come.

Estrela, when her turn came, performed a rite fraught with calamity. Though the words she uttered were identical to those of her younger brother, the force with which they were delivered, along with the vehemence of their cadence, greatly upset the delicate balance of forces in the crowded chamber. A palpable strain in the ether reached from one end of the basement to the other. At the midpoint of the ordeal, during a potent hymn to the anima mundi, a violent sweep of the arm sent one of the candelabras toppling headfirst into the curtain. A minor fire was narrowly avoided, the celebrants all the while maintaining their ritual solemnity. The final bell tolled like the shattering of glass, its jagged echo wafting through the darkened cellar like the cry of an unsettled bird of prey.

Marino seemed to put things right again, with his natural air of grandeur and his measured elocution. By the time the last of the rites was complete, something essential seemed to have shifted within all three of them. They ascended the winding stair into a place that was no longer so familiar as it had been just a few hours before. The house felt subtly changed, the shadows fell at peculiar angles, mirrors glared suspiciously from their gilded frames upon the walls. A noticeable tension had descended upon the intimate interiors. It was as if the rooms and corridors, having emerged from the grip of a lifelong torpor, seethed and trembled with forces and powers that were entirely unknown to them.

Each of them retired to their chosen rooms with little fanfare. "It's important that our chamber doors remain locked until the sun comes up again," insisted Estrela. "The forces we've invoked, having no place to disperse to, must be compelled to consecrate our bodies as we sleep."

Marino, being the most sensible among them, chose a guest bedroom located on the second floor. The décor was far from inspiring, which suited the austerity of his purpose. Silvestre opted to lock himself within the confines of the downstairs library, while Estrela elected to sleep in Esteban's private office. Marino was not entirely pleased with his sister's choice, yet he knew it would be improper for him to object. Each retired to their separate temples with a single taper in a silver candle holder, the flame of which was to persist undisturbed through the remaining hours of the night.

Silvestre's dreams that night were frequented by an ever revolving cadre of undercover civil servants and agents provocateurs. He was pursued by flickering shadows through a series of winding alleys in a city forsaken by its administrators. Narrowly avoiding capture, he slipped into the cover of a forest replete with towering alders and menacing elms, passing ever further into its depths as if in search of absolution for some unnamed crime. At length, he came across a house of ill-repute run out of an elegant chateau in the heart of the woods. There, he gained employment as an accounting clerk, arranging documents and records in a tiny office that looked out onto the banks of a river. The establishment, so he came to find out, had not been frequented for several centuries. Shortly after he began to ply his trade a man in military attire arrived seeking the services of the house.

This man was decorated with an intimidating array of honors and medals. He'd served as a general in the recent Rif rebellion, and was more advanced in years than both Silvestre and his father combined. He made reference to a secret war between the angels and the diplomats, each contending for the influence of the Spanish throne. King Alfonso himself had disappeared some time before, embarrassing his court and baffling his few remaining loyalists. The man intended to secure Alfonso's reign in absentia through a complex sequence of strategic acts of pleasure.

Silvestre lost no time at all in drawing up a contract. By the meticulous illogic typical of dreams, he was endowed with all the expertise required by the delicate matter. Negotiations were carried out with the aid of compasses, pendulums, protractors and water tables. The entire process hinged upon a lengthy expedition through the woods at night. The client-to-be identified himself only as 'The Patron'. He donned a monocle before taking leave of the chateau, casually remarking, as they passed beneath the flaming torches of outer court, that the forest was impenetrable to him without it.

They passed through a long colonnade of imperious oaks, their tangled branches inundated by the residue of night. The canopy of leaves and branches that swayed above their heads revealed only the occasional patch of starlight. The Patron took the lead, guiding them ever further toward the central pivot of the labyrinthine forest. The murmur of the distant river never left them for an instant. After several hours had gone by, the pair emerged into a meager clearing. The space was lit by an expansive trellis hung with red carnations. The garish flowers emitted a phantasmal glow, bathing the entire area in a soft haze of luminous crimson.

In the center of the clearing was found the missing king himself. He sat with rigid spine in a rattan chair that bore only the vaguest resemblance to a throne. His body, swathed from head to toe in majestic robes of vivid scarlet, appeared to have been carved from onyx. His eyes flamed with a fierce regard beneath a glittering, obsidian brow. He appeared every bit as regal as could be expected from such a high-born man. Silvestre bowed low before him, rising with a gesture known to him only by the skills of his trade.

Alfonso spoke, addressing Silvestre alone. The Patron, for his part, seemed somewhat lost in the small clearing. It was difficult to ascertain if the body of the king was invisible to him or if the venerable man had simply decided to ignore it. "The Spanish throne is yours," announced the sovereign. "I've ascended to a greater monarchy and can no longer be bothered with it. You will be duly instructed in the proclamation of royal edicts and other matters of official decorum. May God endow you with the nobility attendant to the office."

When Silvestre finally woke, he was menaced by an unshakable feeling that he was an impostor in his own house.

The sun had not yet risen. The light of his candle, which had nearly been consumed, shed a shimmering film of sepia across the books that lined the library shelves. The faces of his elder siblings passed briefly through his mind. While he didn't for a moment doubt the blood that bound them, he'd felt increasingly estranged from both Marino and his father in recent years. It was as if the loss of his mother had subtly divided her survivors against each other. He couldn't quite escape the notion that his side was somehow tainted.

A single window looked onto the grounds outside of the manor. Silvestre moved the candle to the windowsill, seating himself in a wooden armchair within the shifting sphere of light that it cast. He spent the remainder of the early morning meticulously penning an account of his dream in the pages of a black notebook.

Marino rose as the first rays of sunlight announced their presence through the windows of the guest bedroom. He'd slept not in the bed, but on the floor, having nothing between his body and the floorboards but a faded carpet that barely spanned two-thirds his length. He performed, from memory, a lengthy adoration of the rising sun, at the climax of which he struck a match and lit a tall white taper. This he placed behind a makeshift veil—a sheet of rough silk that hung over the front of the writing desk—thus concealing the light of the candle until a later time.

Having performed his initial task for the morning, he stepped over to the window by the desk and looked out over the gardens behind the house. While these were once elaborate and well-tended, they had since fallen into a state of pitiable neglect. They resembled nothing so much as a war-torn ruin adorned with sickly-looking trellises and overgrown ivy. A dismal little fountain, half-filled with foetid water, stood like an altar in the midst of the haphazard arrangement. While a great deal of effort was expended to keep the front of the house in order, it was inconceivable, between the four of them, that the same could be done for the back. Their father had simply let it go, removing its upkeep from their list of chores. Seeing no reason to delay his work any further, Marino took himself to the center of the room and sank back to the floor, immersing himself in a laborious series of formulaic prayers.

He felt certain that his strategy was unassailable. From the scaffolding provided him by Gikatilla, Abulafia, Moses de León, and a handful of others, he would erect a house within the subtle substance of the invisible. His bricks would be sculpted from the letters of the Hebrew tongue, ecstatic prayer would be his trowel. The permutation of the names of God would be employed to fashion symmetries and aberrations through which the mysteries of creation might be revealed to him. The house would be so constructed as to direct him, by way of an architecture derived from the measurements of the Throne, toward the uncreated fire of transfiguration contained within the central chamber.

Estrela hardly slept at all in the hours that followed her opening rite. Her body was aroused as if by an electrical current, the flow of which ran back and forth between her solar plexus and her brow. She seemed to carry with her an intoxicating inward light that made sleep impossible. After lying on her back on the office floor for an unimaginable period, she finally rose, lit the wick of her reading candle, and took herself down to the pantry. There she found eleven eggs awaiting her in the larder. Two were put aside for breakfast, while another was taken back upstairs.

She placed the candleholder on her father's work desk, which had been cleared of the books and papers that had previously concealed its surface. The flame illuminated a page of *The Magus*, which lay open to a chapter in its latter half. A long title appeared in a font at once stately and restrained. The candle flame caressed the tall black letters as if to coax whatever ghost lay trapped within them to tangible appearance: *"OF THE NAMES OF SPIRITS, AND THEIR VARIOUS IMPOSITION, AND OF THE SPIRITS THAT ARE SET OVER THE STARS, SIGNS, CORNERS OF THE HEAVENS, AND THE ELEMENTS."* To one side of the substantial tome lay several sheets of paper. Upon the surface of the topmost sheet had been scribed the names of eight and twenty angels in two lengthy columns, along with the titles of their lunar houses according to the Arabs, their corresponding sections of the zodiac, their colors and fumigations, their cryptographic sigils, and a single word to encapsulate their natures. The pages that lay below were almost entirely covered with handwritten notes, litanies, and supplemental prayers.

By the time the sun came up, Estrela had immersed herself in a string of strenuous consecrations; one each for the fire, the water, and the holy oil, as well as for the lamps and for the space upon the floor in which the coming ceremony was to be performed. A circle was drawn upon the floorboards in chalk, its circumference limned with names of the Holy One written in Hebrew with crosses between the letters. On one end of the circle appeared a triangle with equal sides. This, too, was protected by the epithets of The Creator. With a bottle of dark blue ink and a weathered paintbrush, she adorned the egg with the name of the spirit she wished to attract. A magical seal was added below in as steady a hand as she could manage. The fumigations presented somewhat of a challenge, with the gardens in the shape that they were. In the end, she settled on a piece of willow bark. This she would suspend above a candle flame by way of an elaborate contraption made from utensils she'd gathered from the kitchen.

The preparations had been completed by the time the moon was visible in the sky. Estrela dined on the eggs she'd set aside along with a few meager slices of unbuttered bread. She sat herself in front of one of the two office windows, letting her gaze rest on the lunar orb. Its radiance was just past fullness. Reciting a formula under her breath, the meaning of which she hadn't a clue, she willed the moon's pallid rays into the secret chambers of her body. An hour passed, perhaps a little more, before she felt sufficiently permeated by the silver light. Having no other official tasks to tend to, she rose and began the first of her conjurations.

She passionately entreated the angel *Kyriel*, the celestial ruler of the lunar mansion known as *Al-Na'am*. Using a modification of 'the invocation of good spirits and angels' found in Barrett's book, she bid the heavenly messenger to appear before her in the triangle. She paced the circumference of her circle from the inside as the litany proceeded. Her hands traced complex sigils in the air before her. As her prayers increased in fervor, her ardor was transmuted into genuine devotion.

She realized, as pungent clouds of smoke rose from the burning willow bark, that the herb would have burned far better had it first been ground. In any case, her consecrated egg was thoroughly suffused with the acrid perfume. After forty minute's work, the angel at last made a furtive appearance. It could just be discerned, not physically but with the mind's eye, some distance above the triangle. Its phantasmal form mingled with the rising streams of incense smoke. The spirit was unquestionably female. Two slender white arms emerged from the luminous folds of a silken cloth that spiraled around her body. Delicate stalks of lily of the valley lay enclosed in her grasp, while her mouth was concealed beneath the open petals of a white lotus flower. Two impassive eyes gazed down upon Estrela beneath a hanging jewel on her brow. The pearl shone like fire in the darkness, emitting a penetrating glow that passed well beyond the limits of the circle.

Estrela remained rooted exactly where she stood, repeating a string of epithets of the goddess Selene in a hushed voice. It took her several moments to remember precisely what it was that she'd hoped to accomplish with the rite. The list of demands that she'd prepared for the spirit was short and to the point: to open the gates of the invisible, to reveal to her the hidden symmetries of the house in which she lived, to allow her to pass into those hidden reaches of the manor which were impenetrable to her senses. Her father's house, she reasoned, was a microcosm just like any other. It must contain, if only in reflection, the long sought-after key to the eternal treasury. By means of subtlety, and by the use of arts whose existence was denied by the authorities of the day, she ought to be enabled to breach its secret recesses and extract a fragment of the crown.

When her petition was complete, she simply stood her ground, hardly prepared to deliver the prescribed string of curses and threats if the spirit got out of hand. She was pleasantly surprised to find her subtle vision increasingly awash in a glow as pallid as the moon itself. The luminosity resided just behind her brow, as if a mirror had been erected there and a light shone on its surface from an unknown source. By shifting her attention inward, she was able to discern the first faint traces of a reflected image.

As the scene took on greater substance, she recognized an area within the manor. The details coalesced to reveal the stairway that led up into the attic. The décor and furnishings were saturated with a rich bouquet of memories that stretched back to the early years of her childhood: blue and white floral wallpaper, a low stand of carved wood that resided in the crook of the stairs, an oval mirror in an ornate silver frame—each element resided perfectly in its place as if she were witnessing them with her physical eyes. The details appeared with greater precision as she focused in on one feature or another. Thus, the texture of the wooden rail that rose above the mirror displayed itself with crystal clarity as soon as she made it the object of her attention.

A shadow fell across the lower stairs. Estrela identified the thick white fur of a Mongolian fox as it furtively made its way down from the upper regions of the house. Her attention was so taken with the animal's sudden appearance that she scarcely remembered where she was. The stealthy creature stepped onto the corridor landing and turned to probe the shadows toward the far end of the hall. As it proceeded into the space beyond, so did Estrela's point of view follow behind it. She moved without volition as if pulled on a clothesline, drifting past petite framed portraits of near and distant ancestors that she'd never once encountered in person.

Having passed through the open doorway at the end of the corridor, they proceeded along a route that far exceeded the boundaries of the house. They slipped through narrow crevices which opened in the wallpaper, doorways meant for servants that hadn't occupied the house for decades, and passageways illuminated by tall, stylish bulbs stained yellow with unsavory substances. Windows without glass in a variety of shapes and sizes looked onto winding stairs and decorative antechambers. The animal continued with a nervous step as Estrela drifted ever behind.

At length, they wound up in a substantial chamber, its walls and ceiling betraying an intricate map of cracks and blemishes. A man advanced in years and attired in impeccable uniform awaited them in a deserted corner. Both hands were clasped upon the handle of a silver cane. Several stars of precious metal were displayed upon his breast below the resplendent gold of his epaulets. The fox approached the officious looking man, who lowered himself down to the unfinished floorboards. He placed a hand upon its head between its sprightly ears and affectionately scratched its fur. His touch produced a marked docility in the animal. It sank to the floor and lifted its snout as if in adoration of its master.

Estrela let herself take in the furnishings of the room, honing in on each element in order to discern its fine details. She observed open cupboards filled with fabric of various colors and materials, wall racks lined with spools of thread and coils of measuring tape, a sizeable wooden trunk that supported a sewing machine so old that she hardly recognized it, and several cabinets containing scissors, needles, and spare machine parts. A work table stood against one wall, covered with the featureless torsos of a variety of dressmaker's models. The man in uniform appeared perfectly at home in the industrious environment. He turned his gaze up to his observer, his white mustache and irascible eyes displaying the indignities of a man of long and arduous experience. "The little bitch can fit into rifts and doorways so small that we can scarcely comprehend them," said he. It took Estrela a moment to realize that he was referring to the fox. "Thus is she enabled to retrieve things that reside in places inaccessible to us. Her expertise is crucial to our operations."

As she looked upon the scene in silence, hardly understanding, the man reached into a pocket and retrieved a narrow pipe. Estrela recognized it as a whistle only after he'd put the instrument to his lips. A staggering silence ensued as the man's cheeks puffed out. The fox at his feet curled up and went to sleep as if entranced by a frequency beyond the range of human hearing. The instrument produced a similar effect upon Estrela herself. She suddenly felt intolerably drowsy and unfocused. Her point of view was pulled in several different directions as the tailor's chamber and its occupant slipped away from her. Her attention was returned, with an unpleasant rush of vertigo, back to her physical surroundings in her father's office. Taking a moment to regain her bearings, she found the circle to be as settled as a tea-room at midnight. The presence of the spirit was nowhere to be found. Quickly, and with no great ostentation, she uttered the license to depart and performed the closing benedictions. The egg was taken from its support, placed against a heavy book upon the surface of the work desk, and covered with a spare pillowcase. Once everything had been returned to order, she opened up the windows and let the mild wind of early spring disperse the heavy fumes of incense that remained.

Marino, meanwhile, having calculated the solar hours, removed his candle from behind the veil at the precise moment that the sun reached its nadir. Thus did he entice the sun of midnight, that it's unseen luminescence may take flame within the lamps he'd placed throughout his mansion in the aether. This, in turn, lent substance to the corridors and chambers within, fixing the volatility of the subtle currents by which the house had so painstakingly been constructed. It was only thus that he was able to sleep with full confidence that his creation would persist throughout the night.

The three of them had agreed to meet in the front parlor on the following morning, there to deliver a brief report as to their progress in the work so far. Estrela had woken shortly after dawn. She rose without ceremony and took her consecrated egg up to the foot of the stairs that led to the attic, concealing it in the corner beneath the low stand where few eyes were likely to pry. She made a mental note to dispose of it before its noxious effusions attracted the attention of the others.

From there, she took a languorous route to the ground floor of the house, traversing a mesmerizing sequence of ornate carpets, narrow stairways, little-used servant's doors, and dark, polished floorboards. A small army of crows had gathered along the rail of the balcony outside the northern parlor. Their contentious cries pursued her down a corridor lined with niches, each of which contained a minor treasure that her father had brought back from one of his frequent trips to Tangier. At last, she stepped beneath one of the three tall arches that led into their meeting place. Marino stood facing the picture window with his hands behind his back, while Silvestre resided on the floor before a wicker chair, his head leaned back against the seat as if in examination of the high ceiling. The insolence of his pose betrayed the general ambivalence that he'd increasingly assumed in recent years. Estrela sat herself upon a seating bench before the fireplace. By the time her older brother finally turned around, she was dying to retreat upstairs again and return to work.

Her report was not overly lengthy. While she recounted the conjuration of the lunar spirit in some detail, she omitted the vision that followed. There was something about the tailor's room, along with the man she'd met there, that she felt was too intimate to relate. She merely stated that something of interest was revealed to her, without mentioning what it was. This was met with no objection from either of her brothers. They'd agreed from the outset to limit their reports to the most superficial details of their work. Silence, they all knew, was among the most potent of the weapons in their arsenal.

Marino delivered a comprehensive account of the frequency and duration of his exercises. While he gave some indication as to the methods he employed, he was cautious not to divulge too much. Silvestre, when his turn came, claimed that nothing of his work could yet be spoken of in any way. He would elaborate further, so he promised, as circumstance permitted. The truth was that he hadn't yet settled on a working method. From the beginning, the prospect of mystical awakening had struck him as somewhat dubious. If such a thing existed, it was the concern of men and women that were far more holy than was he. He merely wanted to explore the Mysteries to whatever degree he was able. He'd read passages in Apuleius and Dante, along with a selection of more modern literary works, which had enticed his imagination. He would be more than satisfied to pass beyond the veil of the sensible world and retrieve the least of the treasures from the region beyond.

He'd spent nearly the entirety of the previous day cloistered in the attic, idly paging through a vellum-bound volume of *Melmoth the Wanderer*. Images from the previous night's dream returned to him with undiminished luster. This so effectively commanded his attention that he could scarcely concentrate on anything else. In addition, he was hampered with an unshakeable listlessness that kept him rooted to the sofa.

He returned to the attic after the meeting, having found the downstairs library to be far too familiar. Not wishing to indulge in another unproductive day, he set about considering how best he might occupy the days to come. Nothing that he'd found upon the shelves of Esteban's private library particularly captured his attention, save for a few titles in French that would be too much work to read. In any case, he felt it necessary to chart his own path to the elusive star that the trio had adopted as their *summum bonum*. Already, he'd come up with countless schemes that failed to satisfy his intuition. In the end, he decided that the way into the sanctum lay precisely in his dreams. The rough outline of a plan began to take form. He would imagine himself, with dogged persistence, inhabiting the spaces that he'd occupied in the dream of the abdicated king, so overwhelming his imagination that it would be compelled to return to them as he slept. He saw no reason to delay. He sat upon the floor before the sofa and set about his task with all of the concentrated diligence that he could muster.

His initial effort continued unbroken for little more than an hour. By sheer force of tenacity, he was able to keep his mind from wandering and to ignore the thousand minor aches and itches that assaulted his body, yet he was forced to accept that he would have to proceed in short bursts. He decided to occupy the periods in between with an investigation of the many boxes, packing crates, and trunks that occupied the attic floor. A systematic exploration, he considered, would serve to pacify his restless intellect, allowing him to return with renewed enthusiasm to his practice.

The first thing of interest to receive the benefit of his attention was the heavy trunk that he'd adopted as an end table. It's top was fastened with a lock, yet Silvestre could discern at a glance that the thing was clearly broken. Upon lifting the lid, he was pleasantly surprised. A varied collection of unrelated items awaited him inside. These had been artfully arranged atop a stack of carefully folded linens.

Indulging his affection for lists, Silvestre made a record in his notebook of the more noteworthy among his findings. This he appended, without a word of explanation, to the minimal record of his first practice period, which itself appeared as a footnote to the long and detailed description of his initial dream.

1 rolled up map of Salamanca. 1858. Monochrome. A winding maze of streets and buildings that might be explored for hours on end. Names printed in letters so thick that they're impossible to read.

6 glass bottles of ink:

- 2 black
- 2 crimson
- 1 dark violet
- 1 maroon

1 matchbox decorated with a coat of arms (a 3-branched stick with fleur-de-lis, red and yellow stripes, Catalan crown)—13 matches remain, 1 broken

1 tarnished dog whistle

1 red notebook (containing not a single word)

1 book of Spanish Heraldry

1 faded photograph of a woman standing before three stone arches in the night. Or maybe in a darkened interior—it's hard to tell. The arches give way to chipped brick above. A plaque with a title is set into the brick: *Étoile*. The sole light is provided by a candle held in one hand. The woman is certainly not our mother, nor any other blood relation I know. She wears a light dress with ties up the front. Her dark eyes make her look distinctly suspicious, as if she's up to something cunning or insidious. On the back of the photograph: *Lyon, 1911*

1 white apron with nothing in the pockets

Silvestre felt quite certain that the woman in the photograph was an indication that he was on the right path. A gift from the invisible, he resolved, was not to be taken lightly. Immediately upon taking the dog whistle in hand, he lifted it to his lips and gave a short, sharp blow. The ensuing silence elicited a minor commotion somewhere in the house below. It sounded as if a heavy object had tumbled off a shelf, giving rise to a dull thud as it struck the floor. Such were the acoustics of the attic that he couldn't quite place the source of the noise. He wondered if he'd roused a squirrel that had somehow found its way into the house. Perhaps he'd even managed to startle a rat. For reasons unbeknownst even to himself, he's always dreamed of living in a rat-infested manor. The thought of the infernal rodents scampering about within the walls and beneath the floorboards gave him no end of delight. With little further thought, he placed the whistle, along with the matchbook and the photograph, upon a low bench of crimson lacquer that resided in the shadows by the attic door. The book of heraldry was slipped beneath his copy of *Melmoth* on the floor by the sofa, while the items that remained, being of little interest to him, were left inside the trunk when the lid was closed again.

Thus did Silvestre pass the remaining hours of the day, alternating between periods of work and exploration. Food was not an issue for him. He'd retrieved half a loaf of bread and a jar filled with jam from the pantry the day before. A box containing eggs and milk was due the following day, and there was oatmeal enough to last for several weeks if need be. He had scarcely any need to set foot outside the attic. Already it had become a private residence for him, comprising a country all its own of which he was the single monarch, magistrate, and citizen. By the time the day had ended, he'd added three further items to the surface of the bench: a silver plumb line, a King of Spades that had been cut in half along the horizontal axis, and a petite book of mildly erotic poetry. These were placed in a symmetrical arrangement with the other items on his eclectic altar, thus to facilitate an oneiric mass in which the consecrated host might be consumed while he slept. Excited at the prospect of revisiting the environments and motifs of his dream, he put himself to bed at a relatively early hour, keeping the images from his meditations ever in mind as unconsciousness stole over him.

Estrela spent the better part of the following day in preparation for the rites to come. She had devised a grand design involving each of the seven wandering stars. These she would propitiate from the lowest to the highest according to the natural celestial hierarchy, having begun with Luna and continuing to work her way up to the exalted reaches of the Saturnine sphere. Not content with confronting the final arbiter of destiny, she planned to proceed into the higher air of the fixed stars. There her point of focus would be Alphekka in the Northern Crown, this being the Star of Gnosia itself. The final step in her apotheosis would take her to the Primum Mobile, the first mover of movers, the crystalline heaven of Ptolemy and Dante, necessitating the abandonment even of the icon of her order. In that inner court of pure divinity, she would be wedded to perfection.

Her scheme unfolded over the course of thirteen days, with short breaks in between the more majestic of the workings. In the days to come, the angels of both Mercury and Venus would be duly interrogated, followed by a grand invocation of Helios. The latter would be aided by the recitation of an Orphic hymn over a Eucharist of aged Monastrell. The consecrated blood of the god invoked, she hoped, would exalt her subtle vehicle with the supremacy of the resurrected sun.

In any case, she had a lot of work to do. Seals were painted on thin wooden discs. Petitions and prayers were written and rewritten. Tree bark was ground to fine powder with a mortar and pestle before the consecrations were carried out a second time. When her labors were finished, she departed from the holy place, taking herself up to the stairway near which she'd stashed her talismanic egg. She sat in silent meditation on the lowermost stair in hopes of deepening her understanding of the vision from the night before. After several uneventful minutes had passed, and her anticipation had begun to give way to torpor, she was startled by a sharp rustling sound from somewhere in the attic. The noise persisted for a moment as she opened her eyes. She sat unmoving, her gaze fixed upon the elaborations of the wallpaper that dominated the upper story of the manor. The silence was again broken by the sound of shifting weight upon the floorboards above.

Half-convinced that there truly was a fox up in the attic, she slowly rose and ascended the stairs. On her way to the upper landing, she passed a shallow niche in which resided a statue of The Savior on his cross. The degree of skill with which the piece had been sculpted was fairly negligible. The unfortunate man looked far more irritated than anguished, as if being forsaken by his god was a mere inconvenience. Would that our trials will be so for us as well, she thought, as she climbed the last of the three stairs, opening the attic door as quietly as she could. The sight of Silvestre on his knees before an open trunk nearly sent her tumbling back down again.

"Your entrance could not have been more auspicious," said Silvestre as his sister took a moment to recover from her shock. "I've found something that might be of interest to the both of us."

"You scared me half to death," proclaimed Estrela, one hand held with fingers splayed across her swiftly beating heart. "You might have mentioned that you'd moved to the attic."

"How can you be certain that I've moved?" asked Silvestre, turning his attention back to the contents of the wooden trunk, much of which had been removed and lay upon the floor beside him. "Perhaps I'm merely taking a break."

Estrela stepped into the dim light of the standing lamp that had been dragged to one side of the trunk. She closed the door behind her as its light washed over the low hem of her skirt. Passing behind her younger brother, she sauntered over to the couch and let herself recline upon its faded cushions. It had been months since last she'd laid eyes upon the interior of the attic. She and Silvestre had been fond of sneaking up into its shadowy recesses when they were younger. They'd spent countless hours there engaged in games that they'd invented between themselves, their caprices typically involving an imagined network of saboteurs and secret agents. They staged elaborate interrogations in which one of them would be made to confess to a series of absurd and impossible crimes. Marino rarely joined them. He thought himself above such childish conceits.

"As it happens, I have moved in fact," so Silvestre informed his sister. "I found the library to be stuffy and uninspiring. The attic is the place of true mystery, only I hadn't realized it until yesterday morning."

Estrela lay with her bare feet propped up on one of the armrests of the couch as her brother proceeded to sift through a pile of opened envelopes. They looked to be quite old. The handwriting that had been scrawled upon their surfaces was barely legible so far as she could see. They were decorated with a colorful array of stamps in various sizes, the postmarks bleeding over in ill-defined circles lined with blurry characters. There must have been upwards of twenty of them. Silvestre was arranging them into two separate piles.

As last, every letter having been placed in one pile or the other, he looked up at his sister. "I suppose you'd like to know what it is that I've found," he proffered.

"I suppose I would," answered she.

"They're letters written to our mother," he said, with no change of expression, "by a Capitán Ignace Renaud."

Estrela sat up on the couch, her interest profoundly enflamed.

"I've only read a single one so far," continued Silvestre. "They're written in French, so it took a little work. What's more, the handwriting is so bad that in some cases it's impossible to make out. With a little effort, I think we'll manage."

"Has Esteban seen them?" asked Estrela, immediately realizing the inanity of her question.

"I haven't a clue," said Silvestre. "The one I read contained hints of affection, though it's awfully subtle. There are other things of interest. I think we ought to divide them up between us."

"The three of us?" queried Estrela.

"Just the two of us, for now," said Silvestre. "We can show them to Marino later."

Estrela remained as if frozen on the couch, the incandescence of the standing lamp bathing both herself and the weathered upholstery in soft cascades of golden amber. She didn't know quite what to think. She knew that no amount of effort would suffice to quell her interest, and yet her younger brother's findings seemed to comprise a formidable distraction from the work that she'd committed to. Silvestre, as was so often the case, seemed to anticipate his sister's reservations. "My finding these is no accident," he assured her, raising a single envelope before him. "I think they're every bit as much a part of our work as anything we'll find in the pages of our father's books. We ought to handle them with reverence."

Estrela leaned forward on the edge of the cushion, her bare feet touching the wooden floor. "You haven't come up with an approach to the work yet, have you?" she said with a provocative grin.

"Not true!" Silvestre was genuinely offended. "My strategy chose me, in fact. I knew that it would. Things always work that way for me."

"OK, I believe you," she said. "You don't have to talk about it if you don't want to."

The two remained in mutual silence for a moment, savoring the luxury of the secret shared between them. Estrela was fully cognizant that Silvestre would never have shown her the letters had she not apprehended him in the act of sorting through them. She bore him no malice for his reticence. He'd always had a tendency to keep things to himself. She felt strongly that a person's most objectionable traits were invariably all bound up with their strengths. This was as evident for both of her brothers as it was for her.

"I suggest that we don't discuss the contents of these, no matter how momentous, until our work is done," said Silvestre as he slowly pushed one of the piles toward his sister on the couch.

"Agreed," affirmed Estrela, as she rose to her feet. Her brother rose before her, standing just a couple of inches shorter than herself. She took both of his hands into her own as if to affirm their mutual membership in this most secret of societies. Letting them go, she crouched to the floor to gather up her share of the letters, rose once more, and took herself back through the attic door without another word.

Having again returned to Esteban's office, she allowed herself a brief examination of the envelopes themselves. They were stamped and postmarked from such diverse locations as Budapest and Luxembourg, Warsaw and Milan. The handwriting conveyed a shaky and enfeebled hand, and yet the script was no less confident for its unsteadiness. Her mother's name on the return address was abbreviated—the first initial appearing before the surname scrawled in full. She placed the lot of them, nine in total, next to the pillow beside her makeshift bed. She would limit herself to one letter a night, starting with the topmost one and working her way to the bottom.

The first of the letters bore a stamp from Tunisia. The tiny image found thereon, printed in crimson on pale cream, depicted a profusion of high archways built right into the face of a rock wall. Scattered date palms studded the landscape above, the tallest among them flanked by the flourishes of both Latin and Arabic script. The cliff face was replete with winding stairways and precarious platforms, the openings themselves revealing only darkness beyond. Along the lower edge of the postage stamp appeared the single word 'Matmata', next to which was shown a star and crescent in a petite white circle. The postmark, in this case, proved impossible to read. The letter inside, no more than two pages long, was dated 17 June, 1919.

The missive opened without a single line of greeting, nor did the whole contain an ounce of warmth. The text immediately launched into a brief exposition on the fantastical titles of sovereigns throughout history. Among them, so it claimed, was that of a Burmese king who was known among his subjects as 'The Lord of the Twelve Provinces of Bengal, and of The Twelve Kings Who Place Their Heads Under His Feet'. Three among the many titles of the king of Monomotapa followed: 'lord of the sun and moon', 'great magician', and 'great thief'. This was to be outdone only by His Majesty of Ava, who was addressed both by his subjects and by foreign dignitaries merely as 'God'.

The second section of the letter recounted a little known anecdote concerning a muezzin in Kairouan who, through some careless accident, had managed to lock himself within his minaret for several days on end. Not a single call to prayer was missed, but, between his holy exhortations, the man was burdened with an alarming surplus of idle time. To pass the hours he created several complex strategic puzzles involving grids and numbers which he scrawled in the dust upon the floor. Three examples were given in the body of the letter, though not a single solution was shown. By some complex and unexplained mechanism, so the text continued, the grids fell into the hands of the faithful where they steadily gained in popularity over the years to follow. Over a century later, a learned theologian in Oran declared that they contained the keys to esoteric secrets by which the soul may be made pure.

The letter maintained its impersonal tone to the very end. It read almost like a memorandum intended for an anonymous recipient. Not a clue was offered as to the relationship between the author and the woman to whom he wrote. Perhaps the letter was a declaration of the utmost ardor, only the sentiments were caged in euphemisms and innuendos so subtle that the recipient alone could discern their meaning. "In closing," so read the final full paragraph, "I present you with a short addendum to Baudelaire's immortal 'Litanies of Satan', penned by my own hand upon a sleepless, starless night.

> O infernal monad, ruinous muse, harbinger
>   of blight,
> Your signature is but a cinder smeared across
>   the luminous aether,
>
> O Satan, take pity on my long misery!
>
> O sacred wine of desecration, red poppy
>   floating in a cup of poison,
> Your sweet perfume intoxicates the architecture
>   of the inmost night,
>
> O Satan, take pity on my long misery!

Yours is a palace of clearest crystal, inseminated
  by the winds,
In the belfry sleeps the holy mother of tempests
  and typhoons,

O Satan, take pity on my long misery!

You, for whom the heavens rained artillery
  for forty days and nights,
Yet still your armies stand unscathed, O
  prophet of despair,

O Satan, take pity on my long misery!

Your infamy is unsupportable, O scribe of
heresy and discontent,
Your legacy is a dismal star with blood of
  dark red ink,

O Satan, take pity on my long misery!

You who hid the one true church in the dark
  heart of the earth,
Your psalter is a single page of concentrated
  sin,

O Satan, take pity on my long misery!

Androgyne, Hermaphrodite, Discarnate God
  of Disbelief,

Hear my praises and supplications in your
    cavern of undying light!
Succor me! Enflame my spirit! Bless my vile
    soul with error!
In holiness and holiness and holiness do you
    reside, O Prince of Luminous Darkness."

Estrela carefully re-folded the pages and slipped them back into their envelope. This, she placed upon the floor in a new pile next to the others. For little more than a minute, she lay on her back and gazed upon the wooden shelves that stood bathed in shadow some distance from her feet. Unable to derive an ounce of clarity from the faint play of the light over their contents, she blew out the candle and surrendered to the embrace of sleep.

One story below, in a tiny bedroom located in the northwestern corner of the manor, Marino knelt on the floor before the dim effusion of his own candle. His eyes were tightly shut and both palms rested flat on his thighs before his knees. The position was accompanied by a nearly intolerable degree of pain. In particular, the tops of his feet, which were currently pressed against the threadbare carpet, were besieged by an infuriating ache that reached like a writhing tendril up his shins. The familiar round of cramps had already long since come and gone. In another twenty minutes, his heels would succumb to numbness. As determined as he was to ignore all these sensations, they demanded his attention with an insidious persistence. In the end, he decided that he'd simply have to live with them. The discomfort followed him like a vexatious shadow into the depths of his meditations.

While his body revolted, his mind at least was kept oc- cupied as he wandered through the corridors of his etheric mansion. The meticulously crafted edifice had attained a surprising degree of stability over the course of the preceding day. His method for gaining entry was simple enough. The house had been constructed according to a system, its intricate floorplan adhering to a mathematical sequence involving the permutation of holy names in the language of the Kabbalists. The characters, in combination, were made to correspond with particular architectural details. These were held before the inner eye as the proper formula was recited beneath his breath. Gradually, as the fervor of Marino's aspiration grew, his imaginings took on the quality of a waking dream. The practice allowed him to traverse the mansion's interiors and to explore the elements of its design.

While getting into the phantasmal house provided him with little challenge, finding his way from place to place proved much more difficult. Navigation was nearly impossible inside the byzantine abode. The convoluted layout had a way of confounding his expectations at every turn. Doors that allowed ingress but not egress made doubling back impossible, while many of the chambers seemed to rotate, deterring Marino's best efforts to keep himself oriented. Mirrors not infrequently offered passage from one location to another, often separated by great distances. On occasion, he'd ascend a stair only to find himself inexplicably descending on the other end. What's more, the manor was inhabited. A multitude of personages revealed themselves within the ornate rooms and passageways, each one of whom was implicated within a hierarchy of staggering complexity. They were swept up, to the last of them, in a perplexing morass of complex operations, their true intentions and affinities remaining hidden beneath a web of artifice. Through subtlety and duplicity, and by use of riddles, games, and subterfuge, they provided a formidable obstacle to the deeper levels of the house.

Marino was no more daunted with these difficulties than he was by the war waged on him by his body. With ever-increasing assiduity did he seek the central chamber, applying every measure of discernment to the enigmas that confronted him. Though the task before him was unfathomable, he never gave up hope. The fact that his objective was ingeniously concealed only increased his thirst for its attainment.

A thorough inspection of countless trunks and boxes had yielded three further items for the bench that Silvestre had adopted as his altar. A petite monocular spyglass was found inside of a tiny box wedged in between two suitcases. The device was fashioned from copper inscribed with a floral motif, and fit comfortably within the palm of his hand. He assumed it was intended to be employed from the balcony of the opera, though he couldn't help but associate it with the monocle worn by The Patron in his dream. Upon finding it, he turned its polished lens upon the furthest reaches of the attic, hoping to spy something of interest or significance between the many slats in the sloped ceiling. To his dismay, a general lack of light prevented him from observing anything more enticing than unintelligible shadows.

Next to the spyglass was placed an engraving tool with a bulbous wooden handle. Thus would be symbolically inscribed the signature of the Star of Gnosia upon the subtle substance of his soul. The third item salvaged was a single cubic die carved from ivory, well yellowed with age. Each of the six sides featured but a single dot, a shallow depression that had been neatly carved and inked precisely in the center. His new finds were arranged with the others to form a grid of three by three. Silvestre spent nearly an hour rearranging the pieces of his collection, swapping one with the other until they comprised a pleasing symmetry that he felt adequately represented his aspirations. He had half convinced himself that, with enough scrutiny, they might be made to yield mathematical secrets by which the hidden import of his dreams may be discerned.

In the middle of the lowest row lay the photograph of the woman with the candle. She had something of the furtive muse about her, with her long, dark hair and her eyes concealed in shadow. He had initially placed her picture in the center, but it appeared conspicuously large in the middle of the other items, and comprised a much better fit with its lower half protruding toward the bottom of the bench. The topmost row consisted of the dog whistle, the book of poetry, which, like its counterpart below, stuck out a little bit above its neighbors, and the silver plumb line. The upper half of the King of Spades resided in the center of the square, the engraving tool and the spyglass flanking the monarch like attendants to the throne. The matchbox and the wooden die stood to either side of the mysterious woman who herself seemed to support the entire tableau.

Between his search through the contents of the attic, his minute examination of the letters from the Capitán, his perusal of Maturin's convoluted tale of Melmoth, and his efforts to press further into the landscape of his dreams, Silvestre had entirely neglected to attend the daily progress meetings in the front parlor downstairs. He didn't suppose that his siblings would be troubled by his negligence. Nobody had come up to retrieve him after all, and when, the day before, he'd passed Marino on the stairs on his way down to the pantry, his absence wasn't even mentioned. He was so occupied with the minutiae of his tasks that only the pressing need for food could seduce him from his retreat.

After three days of persistent work, his dream life finally blossomed. Up to that point, his visions had yielded only fragments of the imagery he sought for. A red carnation bloomed, during a brief hypnagogic sequence, among the refuse in the garden behind the manor. On another occasion, in a dream only half-remembered, the shadow of Alfonso was cast over the carpets in the southern parlor as the sun went down. After both instances, Silvestre woke filled with remorse, as if his quarry had appeared before him and he'd somehow let it slip between his fingers.

On Saturday morning, just before sunrise, the narrative was officially resumed. The imagery continued to unfold over the course of several nights to follow. Silvestre, in the dream, had accepted the burden of maintaining a double life. His inheritance of the throne, being largely symbolic, involved little more than the perpetuation of a series of royal intrigues. Meanwhile, he remained employed as a clerk at the brothel, the clientele of which had grown to include an ever-revolving company of informers and double agents.

His most prestigious account involved the debits and credits of a man who held a seat within his own royal staff. According to his records, the man was also on the payroll of the country's acting dictator, Miguel Primo de Rivera.

The agent had been tasked with reporting on the activities of the monarch. Reports were delivered to the prostitutes of the house, and were thence passed to a liaison who frequented the brothel during propitious phases of the moon. Silvestre made a habit of intercepting the messages, which were then doctored and replaced with misleading details. Thus did he not only come to comprehend the secrets of the throne, which were never under any circumstances to be communicated to the king, but he also managed to keep the dictator chasing shadows.

Several weeks went by in the space of but an instant, as so often transpires in dreams. Silvestre played out both threads of his life in an admirable fashion, finding solace in the management of the throne as well as in the day-to-day affairs of his clerical duties. The pleasing rhythm of his days and nights was unexpectedly disrupted by a second appearance of The Patron, who turned up at the brothel one evening after a prolonged period of absence. Silvestre had not seen him since his initial encounter with Alfonso.

"Your performance thus far has been commendable," he was told. "The next phase of our operation can now commence." Silvestre was to steal the much-coveted star of the Royal Order of the Seraphim, a high honor that had been awarded to Alfonso many years before by the King of Sweden. The medallion, which was kept on permanent display in the hall of records, was to be swapped with a well-executed counterfeit. It was then be taken to a secret place, where it would be put to use in an official ceremony.

As events transpired, that secret place was the very attic in which Silvestre lay sleeping. Upon a high ledge set into a wall near the far end of the spacious enclosure, behind a curtain of white burlap that hung from the ceiling, was found an unlocked trunk containing the earthly remains of the former king himself. His body was carefully removed and laid out upon a marble palette, the stolen icon placed upon his breast. The angels attendant to the honor were propitiated, being the six-winged beings from the book of Isaiah. A flame was thus ignited within the heart of the corpse, which was transformed from solid onyx to a dazzling crystalline ruby. According to The Patron, the fire would persist throughout the dark night which was soon to overtake all of Spain. Once the storm had passed, which could not be expected for several decades, Alfonso's eyes would open of their own accord. Though his body would remain immobile, the patrons of the brothel would be permitted to consult him like an oracle.

Upon awakening, Silvestre furiously transcribed the contents of his dream into his notebook, taking care to record each detail with all of the subtlety that it required. He then turned his attention to the burlap curtain which, just as in his dream, was found in the back of the attic. Indeed, the high ledge revealed itself, atop of which resided the unlocked trunk. He was able to reach it only by way of an unsteady stand assembled from two boxes. Upon transporting it to the ground and exploring its contents, he was disappointed to find only a rolled up carpet and a box of receipts. A quick search through the papers inside of the box confirmed only that they contained nothing of interest. On a whim, he turned the closed box over in his hands and was delighted to find, inexplicably taped to its lower surface, the missing half of the King of Spades.

After several days of excruciating pain, the cramps that tormented Marino's legs had not abated in the least. Allowing himself a slight break from his more or less ascetic routine, he took refuge in the ground floor washroom. The wicks of two white candles on high wooden stands were set imperiously aflame. The tankless water heater, an inelegant, if practical device, was set in operation. Flickering shadows danced across the blue and white tiles above the bathtub, passing from one side to the other like a flock of swallows as the tepid water was slowly heated.

Once the bath had been made suitable, Marino patiently lowered himself into the steaming basin, taking care not to proceed too quickly lest he irritate his embarrassingly delicate skin. The near-scalding water brought instant relief to his aching knees and ankles. He extended his legs to their limit as the twin flames of the two high candles writhed above as if in holy rapture. Just as the bathwater placated his aching muscles, so the decorative flourishes and tiles of the washroom assuaged his aesthetic sensibilities. Having thoroughly immersed himself in the splendors of a mansion etched in light, he found it pleasing to gaze with his physical eyes upon the humble ornamentation of a well-designed water closet.

The tattered book of Kabbalistic excerpts that he'd chosen from his father's library lay face-down on a dark wooden bench to one side of the tub. Several bookmarks protruded from its upper edge, marking the locations of key texts or particularly poignant expositions. When his meditations exhausted him, he would peruse the mysteries derived by his predecessors from the transposition of Hebrew letters, the ordering of the permuted names of God, the architectural anomalies of paradise, and the enigmas attendant to the intrigues of the angels. On occasion, he would find a clue that would allow him to unravel one of the many tangled threads that plagued him in his mansion.

Within seconds, thoroughly relaxed by the water, he had allowed himself to drift into a light and tranquil sleep. The darkness that surrounded him was tinged with subtle luminosity. The house of his inner vision immediately began to formulate before him. Its opulent furnishings and wide arches enclosed him on all sides like a vestment woven of the breath of the Holy One. He had so entrained himself to find his way into the intricate labyrinth that he no longer needed to extend the slightest bit of effort to do so. He had no clue as to his location within the interior of the place. His entrance, in this instance, was entirely undirected.

The rooms and corridors of the serpentine mansion were generally comprised of a fixed set of features, each arranged in different combinations like the values of a mathematical equation. Some of the doors and archways were decorated with numbers, others with mystifying phrases, while the stairways featured plaques at the head or at the base that offered keys to what might be found at either end. Complex insignia were not infrequently revealed within the patterns in the wallpaper. Pedestals encased in glass appeared throughout the many parlors and galleries, their interiors displaying jeweled vestments of haunting beauty and allure.

On this particular occasion, Marino found himself drifting down a curving stairway. The golden rails opened onto a quiet little lounge suffused in soft yellow light. A single table of polished oak resided in a corner nestled within the crook of the stair. The chandelier above illuminated the ebony uniform of a gentleman of considerable age that was seated on one of the chairs. Marino had encountered this figure several times before. Of all the personages that frequented the mansion, he was perhaps the most infuriating. The man had consistently managed to outwit him in the name of the security of the house. "Our territory harbors infiltrators that are so pernicious that they would steal into Heaven and pilfer the very name of God if given half the chance," so Marino had been told upon their first meeting, though he was never himself directly accused of being one among them. "We must keep ever vigilant. It is necessary to take every precaution with the secrets of the house. The center must remain protected lest the surrounding walls collapse."

Marino sat himself, in vision, upon the empty chair directly opposite the rather Machiavellian character. The man's epaulets and golden buttons glistened beneath the lights. Two perspicacious eyes gleamed like stones of precious emerald beneath a head of thin white hair. Terse greetings were exchanged before Marino tried a tactic so direct that it could not possibly succeed. "I seek no less than the Star of Gnosia," he said. "I've come to officially request an escort to the central chamber of the house."

"Rumor has it," responded the man, his hands gently folded on the table before him, "that the treasure that you seek lies mysteriously concealed in a seldom noticed antechamber. You need not thus concern yourself with the center of the house."

"An escort, then, I take it, is out of the question?" asked Marino.

"I will provide you with something far more valuable than that," said the man. He reached a thin, white hand between the buttons of his greatcoat and retrieved a silver cigarette case. Inside of the case lay not a single cigarette, but rather a broken piece of white chalk, no longer than half the length of Marino's longest finger. With this, he proceeded to sketch a rough design directly onto the surface of the table between them. He defined a grid of three squares by three, each box containing a number between one and nine with no repeated digits. "Each of the rows and each of the columns share the exact same sum," he insisted, one hand gliding down and across above the design as if to demonstrate the soundness of his premise. "Barring rotations and reversals, there exists only a single arrangement by which the numbers can be distributed without violating this principle. A square of four by four, however, possesses no less than eight hundred and eighty different possible combinations. For a square of five by five, there are over two hundred million. Imagine how much more so for a cube. Now," the man turned his eyes upon Marino's own, "how many chambers might be found within this very house?"

Marino awoke with a start, his body having suddenly begun to slip down toward the far end of the bathtub. He'd read that it was dangerous to transition so suddenly from the depths of vision to full physicality, yet he didn't feel that he'd sufficiently immersed himself on this occasion to pose a real threat. He propped himself into an upright position, keeping his body in place with his feet while his arms rested upon the sides of the tub. The washroom was nearly as opulent, he realized, as were the decorated chambers of his astral mansion. The images painted on the blue and white tiles had seduced his imagination from the time he was a child. The stylized peacocks and symmetrical foliage seemed to come to life beneath the flickering light of the candles. He once hid within this very room for several hours after a particularly contentious quarrel between his mother and his father. His plan had been to lock himself inside indefinitely, allowing the cramped room to become for him a tiny kingdom of which he was the undisputed sovereign. By the time he'd emerged, his absence having failed to attract the notice of a single member of the household, he felt as if he'd somehow claimed the space.

Slender arabesques of light danced and glistened upon the surface of the bathwater. Marino gazed upon them with vacant eyes as he contemplated the fruits of his efforts. He was not entirely satisfied with the progress of his work so far. He felt that he should be closer to the gnostic illumination that the three of them had set their sights on. In little more than a fortnight, his father would return. The administrators of the school that Marino and his siblings had abandoned would be certain to send a letter regarding their unexplained absence. While the mail might be intercepted, the consequences of their retirement from the world could only be avoided for so long. The liberation that they strove for was supposed to free them from all such concerns, yet at the rate that he was going it hardly seemed possible that Marino, at least, would secure the pinnacle of gnosis. For the first time since the inception of his work, he began to harbor doubts as to the efficacy of his method. The mysteries revealed to him in his explorations were becoming increasingly self-referential. He was beginning to feel like a serpent in pursuit of its own tail.

He took the book that he'd brought with him from its place upon the bench beside the bathtub, having taken care to avoid wetting his hands or forearms so as not to spoil the pages. He hoped to come across a clue within the convoluted formulae found inside, some method or principle that would allow him to proceed. The shimmering lights that shone down from above struck the pages with a rhythmic cadence, rising and falling in elaborate arches across the tiny lines of thick black ink. The structure of the book was the same throughout: the left-hand side displayed the original texts in Hebrew, while the right-hand side contained a Spanish translation. Marino idly flipped through Abulafia's *Book of Permutation*, allowing the ceremonious calligraphy to sink into his soul like a handful of seeds in a patch of rich, dark soil.

Just as he had settled on a series of aphorisms highlighting the merits of the veils before the Throne, he was startled half to death by a sudden rattling of the washroom door. The disturbance was followed by a tumultuous commotion that quickly receded into the distance. An involuntary twitch in his shoulder was followed by the sharp jerk of an elbow, causing the precious volume of Kabbalistic lore to drop headfirst into the water.

Estrela frequently returned to the tailor's studio in her dreams. While it was invariably uninhabited, and was subject to subtle variations in layout and décor, the feeling of the place was unmistakable. The impossible room would seem to have insinuated itself into her memories. She sometimes woke with the certainty that as a young girl she had run her fingers along the bundles of colored thread that lined the cabinets, or that she'd spent several hours in her early teenage years marveling at the antiquity of the sewing machines. As she emerged from a particularly limpid sleep on the morning of the 24th of April, she could almost swear that she'd once stumbled upon the studio after becoming lost en route to some other elusive chamber. She found solace, so she clearly remembered, among the familiar textures of the fabrics and the rigid postures of the wooden models. These impressions quickly faded as she returned to full waking consciousness, yet the emotions that attended them remained with her.

The evening before, having consecrated and consumed the solar Eucharist, she'd been granted a vision of the central pivot of the house. The tailor's room itself revolved around the axis, residing at the halfway point between the central and outermost extremes. The latter, being likened to the skin of a fruit, consisted of the physical house itself. Its rotations traced a signature in which the latent nature of the central axis was given full expression. "Thus my soul," considered Estrela, certain that she had yet to penetrate beyond the most superficial layers of her own nature, and these only in small measure.

The two preceding invocations had also shed a modicum of light upon the tailor's studio and its denizen. The angel of Mercury delivered her a complex parable of the tailor himself, while the Venusian angel spoke of marriage and consummation. When Estrela inquired whether her betrothed was to be the tailor, and further, whether this personage was identical to the man in uniform, she was enjoined merely to shed her garments and stand naked in the presence of the beloved. While she was hardly unwilling to

197

comport herself in such a manner, she was left unsure as to precisely how she might proceed. She was just beginning, so she felt, to comprehend the magnitude of the arcana that lay still veiled before her.

It was just before the highest point of the sun. Estrela sat up in her temporary bed and gazed upon the contents of the bookshelf on the far side of the room. She had stationed herself in the narrow space between the back of the work desk and the wall. The nook that she occupied appealed to her far more than she would have expected. It had the nature and character of a secret place. She could be reasonably certain that her father rarely ventured to the further side of his desk. The view of the office thus afforded to her, especially from her place on the floor, belonged to her alone.

A portrait of Alfonso XIII clad in full regalia hung some distance above her pillow. Very close to this, on the opposing corner, hung a print of Goya's *Sleep of Reason*. The dark frames in which the images were set, as with the others in the office and throughout the house, were glazed with a layer of dust. It was a trivial matter to observe that the manor had not been visited by a maid for nearly half a decade. The meager selection of books that Estrela gazed upon had been chosen purely for their aesthetic virtues. The true treasures of the library, if it could be called as much, occupied a shelf between the windows on the other side of the office. The walls to either side of the main space, where she conducted her ceremonies, were decorated with maps, certificates, hanging carpets, and pedestals bearing slightly vulgar statuettes. Her rites were always held at night and illuminated by a single candle. The sparsity of light served to obscure the rather tasteless décor.

Estrela rose, already fully dressed, having no more than the barest plan as to her course of action. While the following night would see her engaged in a conjuration of the Intelligence of Mars, the day before her was left magnificently open. The preparations for the remainder of the week had already been completed. The climax of her series would take place on Friday, 29 April, the day before her father was to return. She and Marino had agreed to forgo any further status reports. They hardly seemed to serve a purpose, and in any case Silvestre clearly couldn't be bothered to attend them. Putting off the inevitable debacle of breakfast, she retrieved the two stacks of envelopes from the floor beside her pillow and carried them over to the opposing shelf. She placed the letters that she'd already read between a series of petite volumes on mineralogy and a bust of Cervantes' aberrant knight. The books, rather tastefully bound in aged brown leather, were held in place between two ivory bookends in the form of Dürer's praying hands. The unread letters were set down on the other side of the bust. She was determined to savor them slowly during the time that remained to her in the office.

The stamp on the topmost envelope displayed the high walls of a Moorish rampart surrounded by a dizzying arrangement of flourishes and swirling borders. A postmark from Tétouan, unembellished and undated, had been impressed diagonally across the image as if to mar its exquisite beauty. The message inside was dated November 1921, and consisted of little more than a single anecdote. Having been thoroughly defeated over the course of several hands of Ronda by a delegate of High Commissioner Berenguer, the Capitán was treated to an exposition of the secrets by which the man had maintained the upper hand.

"Cheating," so the Commissioner explained over a glass of watered-down Syrah, "is no less a distinguished art than that of lovemaking." He went on to explain, according to the letter, that the art was replete with manifold virtues that could only be comprehended after decades of careful practice. There comes a point in the cheater's development, he claimed, in which the act becomes an aspect of their nature. Thus does the practitioner pass into a region known only to the most exalted craftsman. It is essential, so the Capitán was warned, that the aspirant restrict their practice to the most petty and inconsequential matters. Even the slightest bit of avarice corrupts the purity of the art. When a sufficient degree of subtlety has been achieved, the master finds that they can use their craft to infiltrate the interstices between providence and error. While it remains that death itself cannot be cheated, a true adept may thus be enabled to pass beyond the veil of destiny. There, and there only, might they approach the unapproachable.

Estrela carefully refolded the single page and placed it back into its envelope, setting the latter upon the top of the pile to the right of the bust of Quixote. She rose, gauged the position of the sun from the angle of the shadows on the office floor, and wondered precisely what she might do with the hours to follow. She was disinclined to allow herself to engage in her usual activities. Neither did she feel the need to keep herself bound to an ascetic schedule of prayer and meditation. The prospect of a short break rather appealed to her. She paused for a moment to consider her options, became aware that she was absolutely famished, passed beneath a rather trite framed proverb that hung above the office door, and descended to the pantry.

Being sick to death of eggs, she availed herself of a quantity of oats and a tiny bit of chocolate. The kitchen itself was a horrible mess. Not a single dish or utensil had been washed from the time that her father had left the house. Estrela boiled her breakfast among a ruined landscape of egg-encrusted pans and butter knives soiled with jam, elated to be afforded the luxury of neglect. She ate not in the dining hall, but in the southern parlor, on a short bench covered with luxurious upholstery in the shadow of the grand piano. Before her, on a low table, lay three slender booklets with their covers opened and marks upon their pages. These belonged to Marino, whose skill as a pianist was considerable for his age. Though Estrela had only a rudimentary understanding of musical notation, the compositions were as familiar to her as the layout of the manor.

She'd grown fond, in recent years, of reclining on the settee in the evenings while her brother practiced his craft. The strengths and defects of his character revealed themselves in the agility of his fingers and the scope of his musical palate. Estrela particularly enjoyed the easy conversation that followed the sessions. She wished that she could maintain such an effortless relationship with her younger brother as well. Silvestre, as he'd grown older, had become increasingly reticent and solitary. He was like an esoteric order in himself, complete with a hierarchy of secret pass-codes and unfathomable rites. His mysteries, as a rule, were ever kept concealed, though Estrela suspected that, if only they were divulged to her, they would inevitably shed significant light upon her own.

As much as she admired Marino, she couldn't help but engage in frivolous caprices against him. A deceitful streak ran through her temperament, if hardly malicious, which compelled her to add her particular touch in places where she had no business. From inside the nightstand in her bedroom, next to a weathered history of the Spanish postal system, she'd retrieved an unused razor and a canister of glue. She pulled several of Marino's music booklets from the shelf by the piano and lined them up before the fringes of the carpet. With a deft and careful hand, she set about extracting musical notations from one book and pasting them into curious positions and combinations in the others. Thus did she create several whimsical collages that were in no way possible to play. A bass clef might be combined with an inverted quaver or two sharps to create a glyph as enigmatic as a Kabbalistic cipher, while elsewhere an ill-placed time signature would be crowned with two crotchets crossed one over the other. The errata were placed at strategic points within the compositions in the hope of confusing the pianist at the moment of greatest momentum.

After seventy minute's work, she allowed herself to examine the results of her diversion. She was pleased to observe a certain artfulness in the perplexing arrangements and asymmetries that played out across the pages. She tried to imagine what the resulting music would sound like if it were somehow played. She was surprised to find that it was possible to conceive of a range of pitches, tones, and melodies that lay entirely outside of the spectrum of human hearing. Precisely where this range began and ended, and how grand its scope might be, provided a conundrum that eluded her best efforts to discern. Satisfied, she slipped the books back on the shelf, confident that her handiwork would not be detected for several months at the very least.

A quick trip to her room to drop off the razor and glue was followed by a stop in Silvestre's quarters. There, she hoped to effect a series of subtle alterations for no purpose other than her own amusement. It had been several years since last she'd been in her younger brother's bedroom. It was significantly smaller than she'd remembered it. Opposite the bed, between two linen-shaded table lamps that stood upon the far ends of a dresser, rested a large print framed in rough wood. From the oppressive confines of the frame gazed Dürer's miserable angel, the structure above its sullen wings engraved with a numbered grid of four by four. A single tall bookshelf occupied one corner of the windowless room. The shelves were stocked with decorative volumes penned by Matthew Lewis and Jules Verne, Dumas and H.G. Wells, Haggard, Walpole, and E.T.A. Hoffmann, as well as Stendhal and Diderot. Estrela nearly tripped over a low, circular table, its surface concealed beneath an unwieldy atlas displaying colorful maps of Africa.

Two illustrations on fairly cheap paper had been pinned to the wall above the headboard of the bed. It was clear, from the execrable quality of both the images and the stock they were printed on, that these had been carefully removed from the pages of a book. To the left was shown a woman wrapped up in a full-length cloak that concealed all but her eyes. She proceeded through a forest in the thick of the night, her shoulders hunched over and her arms gathered up before her. There was something vaguely criminal about the woman. She appeared to Estrela to be fleeing the site of some perfidious misdeed that she'd committed. Not a single lamp or torch appeared in the scene, yet both the woman and the trees were awash in pale light as if her cloak was illuminated from within.

Estrela couldn't be certain, but it appeared as if the second image portrayed the same woman as the first. She lay face-up on a plain white mattress, her cloak pulled back from her arms, legs, and head, while a horde of black serpents wound their way around her limbs and torso. A particularly vile specimen flicked its tongue above her brow, while still others emerged from her sleeves. The woman hardly seemed to suffer at the behest of her assailants. Her body, rather, writhed in ecstasy; her euphoric lips and eyes betraying the languorous indulgence of a sybarite under the influence of hashish.

The illustrations struck Estrela as an ideal medium for the plying of her craft. The paper seemed just thick enough to conceal a message on the reverse side. She had a bottle of black ink somewhere in her bedroom, and had found, three days before, a tiny brush in one of the drawers of her father's work desk that would be perfect for the task. As she gazed upon the images, she mentally composed a dozen or more phrases ranging from the mysterious to the absurd. The fact that they were never likely to be noticed made the project all the more enticing. She passed beneath the door frame, paused out in the hall, turned, deliberated for a moment, and remained in place for two full minutes. Contrary to the enthusiasm she'd so recently felt, she decided to abandon her plan. Where Marino, being older, was fair game, she couldn't quite bring herself to betray Silvestre's trust in even the most minor of matters.

Slipping out and closing the door behind her, she traversed a short corridor to a mezzanine that looked down onto the main parlor. She continued past the wide double-doors of the master bedroom, shuddering at the thought of trespassing the place in which her father slept. His library was a different matter. There, she felt, he had assumed an affectation that didn't belong to him. Though he was an initiated Freemason, he could hardly be called an occultist. In the space of only seven days, she herself had far surpassed him in terms of genuine occult experience. At least, she had little reason to believe otherwise.

She passed down a short stair and around another corner to the door to Marino's room. She was disappointed, though hardly surprised, to find it firmly locked. From there, she proceeded to the downstairs library, which Silvestre had entirely abandoned. Above a row of low bookshelves with elaborate glass doors hung a reproduction of a painting which, though it had been in the house for several years, she had only recently taken an interest in. Something about her esoteric work would seem to have brought the image to life for her. The heights of paradise were shown in a sumptuous palette of scintillating reds and oranges. Rolling clouds of coral and rich salmon supported a host of adoring cherubim swathed in amber, vermillion, mahogany, and rose. The chief among the angels swung a censer from a golden chain. A torrent of crimson smoke poured forth from its chamber toward the summit of the painting, which itself was dominated by a triangle composed of a fire of white saffron. The four-fold epithet of God had been painted within its bounds, shedding its divinity upon the assembly of Heaven who cavorted below in perfect innocence.

Estrela felt so pitiably far from the magnificence depicted in the painting. Here she was, puttering about in the outermost courtyard, while she ought to be in the royal chamber approaching the throne. The triangular form of the Absolute seemed an adequate glyph for her goal. She let its radiance enflame her aspiration, muttering an awkward prayer beneath her breath in the hope of stirring the wisdom that lay latent in her heart.

After her ardor had sufficiently cooled, she continued to peruse the image. The original painting could be found in the choir vault in the Basilica del Pilar in Saragossa. She was suddenly filled with a sincere desire to make a pilgrimage to the venerable cathedral. She had not the slightest clue how she might get there. Of course, she would have to wait until sometime after her work was finished. It was not inconceivable that Estaban could be convinced to include the location in a family outing. As she had adopted the image as a symbol of her spiritual aim, the presence of the original ought to confirm her attainment. If, that is, an attainment was indeed forthcoming.

Having tired already of her escapades, and having dutifully performed what had become for her a daily act of reverence, she returned to her father's private library and immersed herself in a study of magic squares and talismanic sigils.

Precisely two days after his sister set foot inside his bedroom, Silvestre undertook a brief excursion from the highest point of the manor to the lowest. In the furthest reaches of the basement, before a magnificent hanging carpet, stood four wrought iron wine racks filled with an enticing collection of unopened bottles. Tall standing lamps stood to either side of the display, their curved glass shades, like church bells, casting dazzling rays of amber and carnelian through the decorative cages. A symmetrical arrangement of copper flowers, leaves, and winding stems adorned the wine rack doors, their subtleties and flourishes appearing to caress the iron bars.

The space in which the racks resided comprised an island of cultivation in a sea of clutter and disarray. To reach it, Silvestre had to navigate a maze of upturned sofas covered in sheets, fancy dressers with decorative handles, shelves with elaborate casement doors, and armchairs stacked on top of one another, all while passing beneath a motley arrangement of hanging chandeliers. Thus were the remains of one of Esteban's many failed attempts at generating income. After his wife had passed away, the unpractical man had entered into a period of financial struggle that lasted for several years. He was scarcely able to pay the land taxes on the property, while his debt continued to increase at an alarming rate. At length, he chanced into his current occupation and the household gained a tenuous sort of stability. He'd long since given up the prospect of unloading the furnishings that he'd accumulated. Like the fossils of etiolated ghosts, they blended with the architecture until they'd merged in spirit with the foundations of the house.

From the time he was a boy of nine, Silvestre had maintained an interest in the decorations that adorned his father's wine collection. A moderate examination never failed to unearth a compelling array of evocative images. Esteban was not an authority on the subject of wine, nor could he afford the treasures coveted by the true collector. He had his preferences, to be sure, but his tendency was to purchase vintages based solely on the appeal of the label. In this, his discernment was impeccable.

Silvestre had passed uncountable hours inspecting the ever-replenishing assortment of illustrations and icons.

They dignified the dusty bottles like the pages of a holy book. The most striking specimens remained with him long after the wine had been consumed and the bottle disposed of: a luminous stag with unfurled banners extending from its horns, a nest of rats with their tails entwined in an inextricable knot, an upright egg set aflame upon an altar in a chamber hewn from stone. The latter would appear to be reflected in a mirror. He'd once found a tawny port from Alijó that displayed a royal crown hovering just above an open lily. The image was printed in luminous silver on a background of dark cobalt. Perhaps his favorite had been among the most simple: a square of vibrant scarlet with a small white hare crouching precisely in its center. Below the diminutive animal was found a single word in thick letters of dusky smoke: *Montsant*.

On this particular morning, if it could be called such, for it was nearly twelve o'clock, Silvestre had come down to the cellar for another reason entirely. He wished to find a proper place in which to deposit one of the items he'd found in the attic. He had with him the lower half of the King of Spades as well as two tall white candles in tarnished silver holders. A sequence from his dream of the night before had inspired his self-appointed task. The body of King Alfonso had inexplicably shattered. A horde of thieves, having breached the attic under the cover of darkness, had crept away with pilfered segments of the rubineous corpse. These were sold at exorbitant prices to the servants of de Rivera, who planned to turn them toward his own malefic ends: the reversal of magnetic currents, the shifting of telluric tides, the propitiation and perversion of celestial influence.

The Star of the Order of the Seraphim, meanwhile, no longer being kept in check by the sovereign body, had grown so hot as to be untouchable. It burned right through the pallet on which the king had lain, through the attic floor beneath the pallet, and through all of the intervening floors until it had reached the lowest point in the house, where it could sink no further. Silvestre, upon awakening, was filled with the conviction that, in terms of the geography of the manor, the place in which the star had fallen was symbolically related to the center of the earth. It occurred to him for the first time to question the relation between this star and the Star of Gnosia. Perhaps, he considered, they were as two sides to a single coin. It somehow seemed fitting that, while one half of the card he'd found remain upon his altar in the attic, the other half be taken, at least for the time being, to the basement. Thus, in accordance with the symbolic language of dreams, would his work encompass both the highest and the lowest.

Sylvestre stood before the ever-tantalizing collection of his father's treasures. The sinuous frames of their containing racks had come to life beneath the golden glow of the lamps. The bottles lay supine like longboats safely moored within their harbors. He passed directly to the back, placing the candleholders on the floor to one side. While it was unlikely that either of his siblings would venture into the space during the intervening time before Esteban's return, it still seemed fitting that he choose a suitably obscure location. His fingers fumbled for the latch on the door of the rack nearest the wall. Immediately as the cage was opened, he was subject to the unmistakable sensation of an animal darting over his unshod feet.

He let out a short, sharp yell, jumped back, and nearly collided with the rack immediately behind him. His first thought was to climb the iron bars. He was calmed by the sound of the culprit moving rapidly away from him. Regaining his balance, he swung around and stepped to one side, his eyes scanning the immediate area for some indication of what it was that had crept past him. As much as he had romanticized the prospect of sharing the house with rodents, he was apprehensive at the thought of coming into contact with one. A flash of motion attracted his eye off to his left. He caught sight of a thin white cat midjump between an armchair and a covered nightstand. As quickly as the dexterous creature had come into view, it disappeared again.

How in the name of all that's holy, he wondered, did this cat that he had never once laid eyes on before find its way into the closed wine rack? He assumed it must have come into the house through an unrepaired opening somewhere on the grounds. This seemed all the more likely given the general lack of maintenance afforded to the manor in recent years. It may even have followed the three of them into the basement when they'd come down to perform their opening rites. Again the animal came into view. White feet could be seen swiftly skittering up the stairs beneath the glow of the distant lights. For the life of him, he couldn't remember whether he'd closed the door behind him when he'd come in.

He stood perfectly still for a moment longer. Not a trace of his new houseguest could be discerned. Satisfied that it had moved on to another area of the manor, Silvestre turned around, the ripped card still held tight between his fingers. He began, with great discernment, to scan the labels pasted onto the bottles. He had not the slightest clue what he was looking for, merely a certainty that he'd know it when he found it. It took him scarcely any time at all to find the proper home for his treasure: a dark Rioja with a label of cloudy sapphire. The paper was decorated with a brilliant star shining above a pathetic little church, the meager ornamentation of the latter nearly swallowed in a rolling tide of clouds.

The candles were placed on the floor to either side of his chosen bottle, which itself resided roughly at the level of Silvestre's heart. He retrieved a box of matches from his pocket and set the wicks aflame. It was clear that there was every likelihood that his card would slip from the bottle's surface sometime after he returned to the attic. The prospect caused him no undue concern, so long as it didn't catch fire from the candles. In his estimation, it should take no more than a couple of hours for a connecting link to be established between the subtle architecture of the house and the convoluted narrative of his dreams. Thus would the two contexts be brought into alignment, allowing the influence of his nocturnal life to cast its shadow on the waking world.

With a steady hand, he placed the card upon the image of the church beneath the star. The stellar luminary on the label blazed above the body of the inverted king as if it were the source of his nobility. Silvestre's act was accompanied by a swiftly mounting tension both in the atmosphere of the basement and along the nape of his neck. The latter sensation spread throughout his body, emitting, as it flowed out through the ends of his fingertips, an audible crack not unlike the sudden breaking of an electrical current. He grew remarkably lightheaded in the seconds to follow. Afraid that he might lose consciousness, he lowered himself to the concrete floor. A wave of static was felt to roll through his environment from the back wall to the furthest reaches of the subterranean space. As it faded, it left a high-pitched ringing in its wake, so soft as to be felt more than heard. Its swiftly fading reverberations brought to mind the distant echo of a church choir.

Within seconds, Silvestre was standing again, the last traces of his dizziness having mercifully dwindled to nothing. He was pleased with the outcome of his miniscule rite, despite the slight unpleasantness it had brought with it. The candles blazed below his talismanic object as if to cradle it in two hands of shimmering flame. He briefly considered spending the night in the basement, but in the end gave in to his intuition, which urged him to return to his station in the upper reaches of the house. He took himself to the top of the stairway and switched off the lights. The last thing that he saw before he closed the door was the shifting and contorting of strange shadows in the distance. Their twisted forms resembled a company of Rabbis engaged in holy dances.

The sacerdotal fires that flamed within Estrela's heart had made her restless and unsettled. She could hardly lay still for more than a minute. She was vexed by a desire for feelings and sensations that she couldn't quite identify. The ministers of Jupiter had been duly called forth, their sigils traced in winding trails of incense smoke, and the resulting insomnia endured beyond the limits of tolerance. In the wake of the holiness that had been visited upon her, she took to wandering without aim through the darkened corridors of the house.

She carried a candle to illuminate her idle steps, her free hand clutching a glass of what remained of the Monastrell. As she approached the doorway of the southern parlor, she found a trace of the stimulation that she so ardently craved. The sound of the piano, played so softly as to be barely discernible, reverberated through the hallway like the warble of a sleeping siren. Estrela immediately recognized the characteristic affectations of Marino's skillful hands. She assumed that he was playing as quietly as possible to avoid waking Silvestre or herself. The particular piece he played eluded her, though she could swear she'd heard it before. She crept up to the doorway, remaining just out of view so as not to disrupt her brother's efforts. Several minutes passed before she identified the composition: it was the 'Ondine' section of Ravel's *Gaspard de la nuit*, though it was played so slowly, and with so many mistakes, that it was nearly unrecognizable.

Estrela was familiar with the music from one of the gramophone records owned by her father, but had never heard Marino play the piece before. It laid a ways beyond his skill level, as was evidenced by the clumsiness of its execution. There was something particularly haunting about the way in which his fingers stroked the keys. The effect was only accentuated by the frequency of misplaced notes and the slight deviation of the melody. The piece proceeded like a river having overflowed its basin, its waters running in an uneven procession along courses they were never meant to follow.

After listening intently for several minutes, she proceeded into the parlor. The light of her candle was overwhelmed by the glow of the overhanging lamp. "I was wondering when you'd get around to coming in," said Marino, his fingers continuing to strike the keys, though at an even slower tempo than before. The music, now that she could see it being played, seemed to convey a subtle hint of self-destruction. She couldn't shake the notion that the way in which he played it somehow wounded him.

She took herself over to the settee and placed the candle on an end table. Marino looked like an exiled prince sitting on the white piano bench—noble, distinguished, and marked by a not unfamiliar resignation. His fingers slowed their tempo to an even greater degree than before, the music rife with fumbles of an almost comic nature. Estrela could see that he was trying to amuse her now. At length, the demonstration came to an end and Marino turned to face her.

Estrela placed her hands together, uttered a dry "bravo," and offered her brother a sample of her wine. He rose and joined her on the settee, taking the glass into his hand and staining his palate with the dark, red liquid. The Monastrell was then passed back to Estrela, who raised the edge of the glass to her lips and sipped in silence. An unexpected intimacy accompanied the act, as if they had partaken together of a sacrament.

"Shall we have a status report?" offered Marino.

"I don't see what we stand to lose by it," returned his sister, sensing that the same misgiving afflicted them both. "I think it's fair to say we haven't a chance of achieving our original aim. It was absurd to think that we could possibly attain to something so lofty in so short a period."

"But we will attain to something," insisted Marino.

"Have you already?" asked Estrela, the bowl of the wine glass gently resting between her fingers.

Here, Marino paused. It wasn't clear whether he hesitated from doubt or simply out of a disinclination to reveal something he ought not to.

"I think I can say that I have," continued Estrella. "Though I couldn't tell you precisely what it is."

She took a sip of wine and turned her gaze toward the bookshelves. There, on a low table before a curtain of rough silk, stood a framed photograph of a man in what she supposed was the regalia of the Freemasons. The man appeared so self-important with his gloves, sash, sword, and apron. She wondered at the minor mysteries that he'd sworn to keep veiled in secrecy.

"Three rites lay yet before me," said Estrela, as if in defiance of her brother's reticence. "If there's the slightest chance that I'm to perceive a glimmer of the crown, it lies in the last of them."

"To be quite honest," replied Marino, "the glimmer of the crown seems to have eluded me entirely. If anything, it seems to taunt me from afar. Like yourself, I feel that I've been given something of worth, and also like yourself, I haven't a clue what it might be."

Estrela couldn't think of a single suitable response. She merely sipped her Monastrell in silence, passing the glass to her sibling at what seemed like appropriate intervals. Fragments of the vision she'd been granted a few hours before still flashed before her mind's eye. After an excursion through a narrow passage that had previously escaped her notice, she'd passed into a ruined church located deep within the bowels of the house. Having found her way into the basement of the holy place, she was confronted with an aged matron. It was she, so sensed Estrela, who had long ago laid the initial stones on which the manor had been

215

built. The two engaged in a transfer of official deeds and titles. They swore their solemn oaths before a vast stone pillar that rose up through the church and into the darkness above. Its surface was engraved with the insignia of an ancient priesthood.

After remaining for several minutes in a not unpleasant taciturnity, Estrela was given to a perverse impulse. "Silvestre has moved the base of his operations to the attic," so she informed her older brother. "He's managed to find a collection of letters that are of interest to us both. Can you guess to whom they're addressed?"

"I'd rather you just tell me," said Marino.

"They're addressed to our mother," said Estrela, the diminishing flame of the candle tracing phantasmagoric shadows along one side of her face.

Marino appeared to be vaguely perplexed, as if he recognized what she was saying, but couldn't put her meaning into its proper context. "Are you talking about the letters from Capitán Renaud?" he asked, after a pause.

This was the last thing that Estrela had expected to hear. She was genuinely shocked. "You know about them, then?" she asked, failing to hide her surprise.

"Well, of course," he replied, still confused as to her point. "Didn't you?"

The conversation was interrupted by a minor disturbance from the direction of the piano. Estrela turned her head in time to see a flash of white disappear into the shadows along the back wall. The ghostly figure re-emerged a second later on the bench before the open instrument. A discordant peal rang out as a flurry of paws made contact with the keyboard, indifferent as to whether they struck the black keys or the white. The unruly feline scampered up to the surface before the empty music rack, its ivory tail curling around the intricately carved wood as it regarded its hosts with a tempestuous eye.

Marino wasted not a second's time. "You know how much Esteban hates the prospect of animals in the house," he said, as he rose from the settee, taking care not to move too quickly lest he cause the cat to flee. "I'd better catch it and put it outside."

Estrela remained exactly where she was as her brother edged toward the piano. Before he'd reached so far as the carpet, his quarry dropped down onto the floor. The cat made its way along the back wall past the gentle emanations of a heating vent, occasionally pausing to examine a wall socket or sniff the silken covering of an end table. As soon as Marino closed the gap between them, it was off again. The pursuit continued through the doorway and out into the hall, the cat maintaining its leisurely pace as if it couldn't be bothered to break into a run.

They proceeded up a winding stair beneath the dim glow of a hanging chandelier, its golden rays casting long, slanted shadows in which Marino lost sight of the exasperating beast. He crept around a corner to a corridor replete with archways, his eyes alighting on a tail above the surface of a low bench. Following his prey into an unused sitting room, he was dismayed to find that it had disappeared among the furnishings. The lights revealed a gallery of sibyls encased in heavy wooden frames, their fingers clutching a diverse assortment of banners and scrolls, whips and crowns, doves, flaming lanterns, and crosses. The flourishes in the wallpaper resembled darkly jeweled daggers with their tips pointed upward toward the ceiling. He nearly lost himself among the sumptuous ornamentation as he searched behind a cabinet lined with ivory busts and open books.

Having all but given up, he'd returned to the corridor, when the sound of smashing porcelain sent him briskly pacing through a narrow servant's door. He proceeded over wooden floors that tilted slightly to the left or to the right, giving way to the conclusion, as he tracked the sound of skittering footsteps, that it would be easier to let the infernal creature find its own way out. The occasional mewling echoed from the distance as he advanced from one room to another. The acoustics of the house kept him constantly disoriented: sometimes the cries hailed from above, at others far beneath his feet. Marino felt as if the cat were mocking him, having recruited an army of its peers to produce the impression that it was able to reside in several places at once. He wound up standing in the darkened foyer, listening intently and having no idea where to turn.

12 December, 1922

L. Azarola,

A confession is in order. I am a man of consequence, and thus I feel that I may speak freely and without fear of reproach. Not infrequently, in the course of my travels, I seek a sort of absolution in the impartiality of nature or in the dispassionate sanctuary of a house of God. Whether in the heart of the Black Forest under cover of the ceaseless night, upon the shores of La Rochelle before the crashing orchestration of the waves, on the nocturnal streets of Ghent in the pouring rain, or in the Basilique Saint-Nicolas or the Cathedral of Our Lady of Valencia, I pray for a particular class of revelation that is only hinted at in the works of the most obscure and overlooked of theologians. There is a knowledge so profound that it subsumes the knower. It acts as an insidious poison to the human spirit and corrupts the very substance of the soul. In so doing, it dissolves the barrier that we ourselves have erected before the mind of the Absolute. That this revelation is not granted me only goes to prove the impassivity of a God so remote as to be impervious to prayer. This causes me a certain anguish, yet I will not bemoan my fate. To give oneself without reserve to anything less than the impossible would comprise an error so grave that it could never be atoned for. Thus do I return, humbled yet invigorated, to perform my daily duties in my field of expertise.

Some time ago, I took a meal in the home of a superior officer. Measures had been taken on the part of my host to avoid such an eventuality, yet circumstances conspired to leave us without a reasonable alternative. I had been duly warned beforehand that the man's elderly mother, with whom he was staying, had been given to a progressive loss of reason. It was a malady that ran throughout his family history, so I was told, a germ in the blood that would doubtless come, in time, to claim his own mind as well. Throughout the evening, he tried his utmost to keep the irascible woman and myself from being left alone with one another. His attempts, however noble in intent, proved futile. As I returned from the washroom after the meal had been served, the mistress of the house pulled me aside and presented me with a confession that I was not soon to forget.

Not a single night passed by, so she informed me, in which she failed to take herself into the expansive woods behind the house. Here she spent an hour or more engaged in the most horrific sequence of howls and lamentations. This was at once an offering, a prayer, and an expression of devotion for a God that could not be named, a gift made of her overwhelming destitution in the face of the ineffable. The stars above turned over in their beds and howled with her, so she said, knowing, as did she, that the absence of acknowledgment was nothing less than the supreme response to their entreaties. She spoke to me of the funeral rites of the ancient Greeks, in which the wails of the mourners, who were employed by the surviving relatives, were thought to guide the souls of the deceased to their final resting places. So, too, if the need arose, might their well-trained voices restore the animating fire to a corpse. These artisans, so she related, had learned their potent craft from none other than the sirens. The latter were once the handmaidens of Persephone, so she reminded me. When the maiden was seized by the lord of Hell, they served as psychopomps. Their intoxicating dirges ushered their mistress through the country of the damned that she might reign within that dismal place as the queen of the shades. This venerable art, the woman claimed, had been turned by theologians, in the intervening centuries, toward a doctrine of secret worship. The aspiring mourner may expect to receive a missive from a temperamental wind, a subtle poison that mingles with the breath and which endows the voice with holy dignities. Thus, and only thus, may the true worshipper address the beloved.

Our conversation was interrupted by my superior, the woman's son. Later in the evening, after she had put herself to bed, I was assured that her incessant ramblings were little but the fancy of a deteriorated mind. She rarely left the house, he said, except to water the garden, and even then she couldn't stand to be out of doors for more than a quarter of an hour at most. I was advised to simply pay her no attention in the hope that she would refrain from lambasting me further. The evening proceeded without event, and we did not speak of the incident again.

Yours in faith and fidelity,

Capitán Ignace Renaud

221

For lack of a reasonable altar, Estrela had erected her lonely candle on a sitting bench that she'd dragged up from the downstairs library. The smoke of smoldering cypress leaves, properly dried and ground to fine powder, poured forth from two small white dishes placed to either side of the flame. For a bell, she'd fetched a crystal decanter from the kitchen. When struck with a long, thin dessert spoon, it produced a penetrating ring that admirably filled the space. The names and sigils of the object of her invocation were scrawled in chalk upon the backs of serving trays, their barbarous epithets spelled out in a perversion of the original Greek.

The opening purifications were performed without the slightest deviation. So cleansed was her father's library after the initial fumigations had begun to disperse that she felt as if it had disrobed before her. The space was humbled in its nakedness, the glow of the candle radiating in its midst like a light left flaming in a catacomb. She felt like an archaic priestess as she petitioned the attendant spirits of Kronos, having taken herself to a place forbidden to her to invoke the influence of unimaginable forces.

The passages of her litany, which she had duly committed to memory, were interspersed with resounding peals of the bell. Her prayer resembled fragments of a testament to a lost empire, being equal parts entreaty, paean, hagiography, and lamentation. Her delivery was imbued with a poetic reverence for the melancholic genius of past ages. Her fervid incantations continued long into the night, taking her well past the point of weariness to the brink of exhaustion. Once she'd recited, several times over, the entirety of the text that she'd composed, she took to improvising hymns inspired by the momentum of the rite. By the time she finally desisted, her impassioned assault had given way to a passivity previously unknown to her. The god invoked rushed in to fill the emptied chalice of her heart until it overflowed.

Two stories above, at that precise moment, Silvestre sat in contemplation of the holy items on his altar. He'd emerged that evening from a particularly inspired vision. A white poppy inscribed with heretical verse had triggered an insurrection in the brothel. The tumultuous event came to a head with the explosion of a mirror in an ancient monastery. Alfonso's remains had been gathered between its ancient, soot-stained walls. The shattered fragments were placed together, bound with a single piece of thread, and stained with ink distilled from the blood of the devout.

Events escalated quickly. Forces were mobilized. A weary populace braced themselves for confrontation. The Patron sent a signal to his acolytes from the confines of a bell tower beneath a fevered sky of ether and ambergris. The Star of Gnosia itself made an appearance, though not in the visible heavens did it shine. Its secret character was revealed within the pages of a book—a furtive volume, written with lamp oil, that had been passed from hand to hand by the adherents of the throne.

The glyph of the star was mirrored in the arrangement of items on Silvestre's altar. Small glass pendants containing pressed flowers had been placed to either side of his grid of three by three. The rightmost displayed a fragment of a musical score upon the backing, while the left, housing a crimson bloom of five frail petals, was backed only with thick white paper. Below the grid appeared a key of slightly tarnished copper which, so Silvestre had reason to believe, comprised a spare for the lock on the door of his father's private office. The final space, above, was occupied by a silver Peseta. The coin was several decades old and featured, on its front side, an image of the reigning Monarch in his younger years. While the worth of the coin was technically negligible, it carried tremendous value for Silvestre—by virtue of its image, and the context into which it was insinuated, it was subtly imbued with the influence of royal blood.

At the moment that the coin was put into its place, a palpable surge of etheric force shot down through the floor. Upon reaching the basement, it flowed back up again, passing through Silvestre's fingers and up through his spine. He immediately grew completely numb, his limbs held fast by an involuntary rigidity. An image of the manor appeared before his inner eye. The floor plan, décor, and furnishings were all displayed before him in exquisite detail. Somewhere in a chamber whose location couldn't be discerned slept the reconstituted body of the King of Spain, the radical effusions that emanated from his crown shuddering through the aether like a magnetic pulse. An abominable tension wracked the foundations of the house as his authority was absorbed into its stones. Disturbances took place at the cardinal points: glassware toppled, a window burst, cupboards flung open and their contents prematurely spoiled. An inexplicable crack disfigured a bust upon a low table in the northern parlor. By the time the turmoil had run its course, Silvestre had regained his sensation and mobility. He felt an unexpected intimacy with the hidden reaches of the manor, as if he'd passed into the chambers of its secret heart and debauched their inmost recesses.

Marino, meanwhile, was comfortably sitting in his usual position in the guest bedroom, his unmoving body bathed in the rhythmic coruscations of a candle flame. A distant commotion had given him a minor start, threatening to disrupt his equilibrium. So cacophonous was the disturbance that he was tempted to get up and investigate, yet the ease of his posture convinced him to ignore it. The pain in his legs had mysteriously abated two days before. Just when it had reached its height, after several agonizing hours, the cramps and spasms fell away and he found himself more comfortable than he could possibly have hoped. From that point on, within seconds of assuming the pose, his entire body passed into an opiated splendor.

The candlestick before him had been placed upon a chessboard, either end of which was occupied with a minor treasure. The futility of his efforts had moved him to seek out alternate routes to the apotheosis he strove for. Since his former strategy had consistently managed to baffle his intellect, he'd decided instead to embrace the irrational. The board before him had once belonged to his father. They used occasionally to play when he was younger, he quickly learning to outfox his superior. The man had grown too busy after the passing of Marino's mother to afford time for such diversions. The child had at first suspected that his father had simply grown tired of losing, and began purposely to throw the majority of his games in an effort to win back the favor of the man. Though this proved to be of no avail, the game board had retained a principal place in Marino's heart.

The chess pieces themselves had been left down in his bedroom. In their place, on the queen squares, sat two precious stones that Marino had inherited from his mother. They'd been taken from a collection of mourning jewelry which was normally kept in an attaché case beneath his bed. The rightmost piece was a pendant of flat black stone set into a circle of gold, an image meticulously painted onto its surface. The goddess Nyx, the ancient matron of the night, appeared in lustrous ivory with two children held against her breast. She was crowned with a diadem of mist and fog, while two shining wings unfolded behind her. Her body was surrounded by the starless sky, a lusterless expanse that lay barren and impassive—yet she, the very substance of the void, offered sustenance to the lost souls that were enfolded in her arms.

On the left side of the board lay a polished opal, its surface engraved with an image of a woman in long, flowing robes. Her arms were thrown into the air above her head, while her face turned toward the heavens as if in surrender to her destiny. She'd given up everything in her despair and was no longer in possession of her senses. As miserable as the image was, Marino had always detected a trace of joy about the shattered woman. There was something celebratory in her posture, as if she exulted in the complete abandon bestowed upon her by her loss. The light from the candle at the center of the board cast shimmering waves along the folds of her robe.

Marino couldn't help but feel a trace of sacrilege regarding the abuse of his heirlooms, though the slight sting of guilt seemed strangely to exalt him. He felt, against his better judgment, as if the fire of his aspiration was excited by expressions of iniquity. This trait had been entirely unknown to him before he'd begun his laborious retreat. It was revealed a little at a time over the course of his meditations. This caused him more than a little disquiet, yet something inside of him, something purely intuitive, insisted that the taint of sin was essential to the attainment of grace. He'd even come to secretly relish the disordered state of his father's house. Never in his life before had he seen it subjected to such disarray.

Closing his eyes and withdrawing his senses, he began the mental recitation of a complex formula. Before the book that he'd taken from his father's library had been irrevocably ruined, he'd found within its pages a long passage devoted to the Shekinah. The text, derived from the Sefer ha-Zohar, had particularly inspired him, leading him to compose an entreaty of his own to the Divine Matrona. He extolled her as the mother of both Heaven and Earth, the exiled glory of the heavenly Jerusalem, the soul of the Temple, the betrothed of the Holy One, and the gate of the highest wisdom. Foregoing his original intent, he abandoned himself to the mercy of the goddess that she may bestow upon him the flower of her Mystery.

As his prayers began to enflame his spirit, he took the twin pendants into his hands and let their essence intermingle with his own. He was certain, as he held them, that the images on their surfaces comprised the key that had thus far eluded him. No sooner had the thought arisen, than a luminous tide overtook him, rolling over the boundaries of his vision and pulling him down into an irresistible undertow. The pallid light subsumed his senses and dissolved the threads that bound him to the world. His single overwhelming thought was that he'd drowned. He was cast adrift in an ocean of fire, certain that both sun and moon had been devoured. He felt so miniscule against the vastness that he scarcely seemed to exist at all. He abided for a moment as an infinitesimal point having neither magnitude nor dimension. Finally, he emerged, as if resurrected, above the surface of the fiery sea. Here he beheld the object of his aspiration: the Star of Ashtoreth, the splendor of Gnosia, the eternal jewel in the crown of Knossos—she stood naked and resplendent in a sky of flaming topaz, her most intimate abodes unveiled. No more than a momentary glimpse was afforded him before the vision rolled back like a receding wave. Marino was left speechless in the candlelit bedroom, clutching the pendants in his sweat-bathed palms like a man in the grip of apoplexy.

Estrela was unable to determine whether she'd slept for so much as a minute throughout the entire course of the night. The sun beamed in through the far window with a grandeur given only to celestial bodies. She felt as if she had become so tenuous that it's light passed right through her. The past several hours had been spent in an exalted state. She'd seemed to hover on the border between un-consciousness and prayer, her body sheathed in a tenuous fire that left her perfectly revitalized. If at any point she'd crossed the hazy border into sleep, then she'd done so in a state of numinosity that could hardly be distinguished from waking.

The entirety of the previous day, with the exception of two short breaks for meals, had been spent in a series of ardent devotions. Fifteen among the seventeen fixed stars listed in Barrett were beseeched in turn, culminating in an extended paean to the Star of Gnosia. Each of them enflamed her spirit a little more than the one before it. They served as revivifying nectars to the soul that had been ravaged on the previous evening by the God of the Scythe. After the final striking of the bell, she was swept up in a visionary baptism beyond anything she'd yet encountered. She passed through jeweled bathhouses of devastating splendor, furnaces and forges housing fires of primal wisdom—at last she emerged onto the shores of the Empyrean, the all-consuming waters rolling up at her feet. The last of her series of devotional rites was to take place throughout the course of the day. The work would culminate, long after the sun went down, in an invocation of the highest god.

A perplexing array of questions remained unanswered. She still had not the slightest clue whether the man in uniform was indeed the tailor, or if the latter was in some way his superior. A significant portion of the content of her visions entirely eluded her intellect. While the enlightenment she'd originally sought seemed unlikely to be attained, she was certain that her work would result in something of definite importance. If nothing else, she'd tasted of exotic fruits that would otherwise have been inaccessible to her.

Determined to avoid any trace of idleness, she rose without delay and took herself before the altar in the center of the office. Slowly, and with great deliberation, she lowered herself to her knees and placed her forehead to the floor in deference to the rising sun. The eye that resided in her heart beheld the majesty of Godhead from which the solar disc took form. There lay the pinnacle of her aspiration: the ancient of ancients, the primal mover, the holy scribe that leaves its signature on every manifested thing. It blazed and scintillated like uncreated fire at the summit of the heavens. Estrela could sense, in its immaculate perfection, the very seat and seed of her own soul.

Her mental poise was grievously disturbed by the sound of three sharp raps upon the office door. She remained exactly as she was, eyes closed with hands pressed palms-down on the unpainted wood to either side of her brow. Whatever the matter was, she hoped, it would cease to be a bother if she simply refused to respond. That hope was dashed as the vexatious knock was repeated with slightly greater urgency, this time accompanied by an insistent exclamation: "Estrela!"

"Go away!" she hissed in a voice of pure disdain. She had already recognized Marino by his knock alone.

"Esteban has returned!" came the urgent reply. "He's in the driveway, talking to his attorney."

Time completely ceased for an instant, though it may as well have been an eternity. "WHAT!?!" she cried, unable to believe what she'd heard. She found herself risen back onto her knees without the slightest volition on her part. An object of some sort, metallic from the sound of it, was flung beneath the door and across the floorboards. Estrela grasped precisely what it was as the sun gleamed on its copper surface.

"Silvestre has managed to find a spare key to the office," so claimed the voice from the far side of the door. "Get everything back to order and get out of there as quickly as you can!"

"Marino," she proclaimed, with self-righteous ire, "if you're joking I will sneak into your bedroom and strangle you while you sleep, I swear it!"

But already he could be heard swiftly receding down the corridor. The truth behind his warning resided like a stone lodged in the pit of Estrela's heart. She knew she had not a minute to spare, yet she couldn't bring herself to vacate her holy place just yet. She closed her eyes and allowed herself a single second of piety, placing her hands together before her breast as her entire body ached with longing. The Star of Gnosia persisted in her inner vision, its timeless rays abiding in the endless night of incarnation. Having given her due to the invisible, she rose to her feet and did what needed to be done.

Her work proceeded at a frantic pace. Barrett's un-wieldy tome was closed and placed back upon the shelf. The items laid out on the floor before the desk were put back with as much organization as she could manage. The blankets were folded into a square, the letters to her mother retrieved. Her ritual items were set on her pillow as she praised the utmost heavens that she'd already wiped up the last of the chalk marks. She snatched up the key with furious fingers as she headed toward the door, her mind racing to remember if Esteban, in his letter, had given a date for his return or merely a count of days. As she stood upon the threshold and swept her gaze across the room, she was moved by an irresistible impulse. The thought was absurd, yet its perversity compelled her. She must leave her mark upon the place—something to indicate, if only in secret, that the office belonged to her and not her father. She was well aware that she ran every risk of being caught in the act. Such a blatant flirtation with danger, she felt, would comprise a sacrament that might almost redeem the interruption of her work.

She stepped back over to her father's work desk and retrieved a pencil from an open onyx box. Moving on to the corner in which she'd slept for the past twelve nights, she took herself before the portrait of Alfonso. She considered Goya's *Sleep of Reason* as well, which hung upon the adjoining wall. The image of the insensible man besieged by owls and other beasts had pleased her ever since she was a child. She shifted her gaze back and forth from one to the other, unable to decide between them. At last, without the slightest plan, she took the portrait of Alfonso from its place upon the wall and set it face-down on the floor. She had no time to consider an appropriate epithet. She simply scrawled, upon the back of the frame, the first thing that came to her mind: "*Dare not to wake, O insensible king, for thy sleep sustains an empire.*"

With great haste, she hung the item back upon its nail and darted out of the office, greatly relieved, upon closing the door, to find that the key did indeed fit in the lock. Piling her possessions into her arms, she swiftly headed back to her bedroom to conceal the evidence of her transgressions. She passed Marino on the stairs, he diligently clutching a broom and dustbin filled with shards of broken pottery. She suddenly recalled something that had escaped her. "The book you'd taken from the library," she pressed him. "Where is it?"

"Thoroughly destroyed," he said. "We'll just have to hope its absence goes unnoticed."

They parted company without another word, each heading off to their own respective quarters. Immediately after dropping her armload onto her bed, Estrela heard the unmistakable sound of the front door briskly closing. "Marino! Estrela! Silvestre! Before me in the front parlor at once!" So penetrating was her father's thin, sharp voice that it carried without diminution to every corner of the house.

Yet a further discrepancy occurred to her as she turned toward the mezzanine. 'The egg!' she thought, as she froze in her tracks—it must certainly be growing more than a little rank by now. It wouldn't do to have her father dig it out from beneath the end table to find that it was decorated with symbols from his own books. It seemed highly likely that she would not have the opportunity to retrieve it before the scent attracted his notice. She would have to attend to the problem now, whatever the consequences.

Doing her best to keep her step as light as possible, she raced up two flights of stairs to the crook in the attic stairwell only to find that the sought-for item had vanished from its hiding place. Doubtless Silvestre had detected its stench and disposed of it sometime earlier. For a single moment, she considered ascending to the attic, there to simply ignore the drama down below until her father came up to fetch her. The absurdity of the thought raised her spirits a little.

She made haste to take herself downstairs, fearing all the while that she'd left some crucial bit of evidence in the private office. As she crossed over the mezzanine, a brief moment of eye contact was established with the man below. He stood, as he so often did, with his spine held rigidly and both hands behind his back. He was dressed in his usual fastidious manner, his raised eyebrows betraying more than a hint of irritation. She emerged upon the lower stair and took her place next to her siblings, both of whom had preceded her by a little over a minute. The three of them stood lined up in a row like soldiers awaiting inspection.

"So considerate of you to join us, Estrela," remarked Esteban, not deigning to look her in the eye as he addressed her. The man who fancied himself the master of the house was anything but an intimidating figure, with his neatly trimmed beard, balding pate, and oval spectacles. His penetrating eyes conveyed the shrewdness of a military strategist, or at the very least a bureaucratic expert. The proficient demeanor that he projected was ever defiled by a subtle streak of poetry that seemed to taint his very blood. He gave the impression of a man caught between two worlds, neither wholly of the one nor of the other.

"To say that I'm a little bit dismayed to see you standing here before me is an understatement of the highest order," he began. "Oughtn't you to be in school at this hour? What's more, the grounds are littered with leaves and debris. I didn't dare invite my guest inside, for fear of the disorder that may have awaited us. As it happens, the inside of the house is in no better shape than the outside— the banisters are choked with dust, to say nothing of the floor. I am perfectly aware, by the way, that you've failed to contact Bonifacio. I suppose you fed yourselves on toast and jam while I was gone?"

"And eggs, sir," piped up Silvestre.

"It's a wonder you haven't made yourselves ill," continued Esteban, his brow a map of furled flesh. "Am I correct in my assumption that you haven't tended to a single chore for the entirety of my absence?"

"Correct sir," affirmed Estrela, making no great show of remorse. "Not a single one."

Esteban turned his eyes at last upon his only daughter. For a single, uncomfortable moment she became convinced that he knew every detail of what had taken place within the house while he was gone. He had a way of wielding an acumen that pierced right through the most impenetrable armor. His own façade, by contrast, was like a polished mirror.

"Don't think that your honesty will absolve you of punishment," he said at last. "A house without justice is a house which cannot stand. I have long endeavored to impress upon all of you the exactitude that runs through every aspect of nature. What you cannot learn with your intellect, you will have to learn with your hands. You will be made to atone for your neglect. There will be quite a lot of cleaning in the weeks to come."

Estrela was already devising a method by which her prayers might be silently delivered while she toiled. She had no intention of giving up her aspirations. If she could not pursue them openly then she would have to work behind a veil. She felt that this was probably for the best in any case—should not the invisible be propitiated in secret?

Her eyes glazed over slightly as her father continued to issue his admonishments. She knew better than to expect undue severity, for he was not an overly harsh man. He was rather like a man comprised of diamond—at once perfectly transparent and maddeningly opaque. Thus, despite the fact that he was nauseatingly predictable, she had always felt as though she hardly knew him.

She wondered if the Holy Order of the Star of Gnosia would continue to exist, or if it had officially dissolved at the moment of her father's return. Might it persist even if none of them spoke of it openly? She decided that it would, at least for her. It seemed to have left its imprint not only on herself, but on the etheric double of the house. She hadn't quite accepted the fact that they'd lost their newfound autonomy, nor that the place was no longer entirely theirs to do with as they pleased. The thought of things returning to the way they were before seemed so dull as to be unbearable.

Esteban's monologue was brutally interrupted by the shattering of ceramic in the near distance. The disturbance sounded as if it came from somewhere beyond the mezzanine. "Just what in God's name is going on here!?!" he demanded.

A streak of white shot down the stairs, dashed atop the sinuous arabesques that embellished the carpet, scrambled onto the wicker chair beneath the gilded mirror, and struck a vexatious pose upon its elevated crest. The contentious feline unleashed a low-pitched growl in Esteban's direction as the fur on its back bristled in the morning light. The chair proceeded to topple over backwards beneath its weight. Unsettled by the minor catastrophe, the beast retreated beneath an archway by the window, vanishing into the shadows as quickly as it had appeared.

"Well, apparently the place has gone to blazes in my absence," remarked Esteban, who had reached the upper limit of his perturbation. "Is there anything else you'd like to tell me or would you prefer I found out for myself?"

Estrela politely withheld comment. She wondered briefly if her father could possibly fail to notice the lingering scent of the incense that she'd so copiously burned in his office. Marino, too, declined to speak. He hadn't breathed a word since Esteban's appearance. Doubtless, he was the only one among them who felt the slightest touch of shame in regard to their collective mutiny. Silvestre, who stood on his other side, was desperately trying to stifle a fit of laughter. His lack of self-control, which nearly inspired the same in Estrela, presented a striking contrast to the somber mien of his older brother.

"You think this is all tremendously funny, don't you?" demanded Esteban, eyebrows raised before his youngest son. "Really, Silvestre, I don't know where you learned to be so obstinate. I leave it to you to track down the infernal creature and put it out of the house. I can only hope to God that you haven't been so senseless as to feed it."

"Consider it done," said Silvestre, having mastered his frivolity. "Sir," he added, after a self-conscious pause.

Esteban, ignoring Silvester's impertinence, removed his spectacles and placed his fingers firmly against his eyes. "In four hour's time, I will conduct a thorough inspection of the kitchen and the pantry," he said, replacing the glasses on his face. "The dining hall and each of the washrooms will be subjected to the same. I expect to find them without blemish and in impeccable order. That will comprise a start. You are dismissed for now."

The three of them dispersed to the further reaches of the house in silence. Having been through the drill so many times before, they hardly needed to confer with one another as to who would tend to what. Estrela followed her younger brother through an arch that led into a well-lit, if somewhat incommodious foyer. They passed beneath the painted eyes of a bishop seated on a bench of gold. The cross that hung around his neck was flanked by half-melted sticks of paraffin which themselves arose from a silver candelabra on a console table below. Estrela took a detour beyond the arch on the further side. There the two siblings, the younger and the elder, parted company with one another to attend to their respective areas of expertise. She would sweep the corridors and wipe down one of the washrooms while Silvestre maintained the kitchen and the pantry, as he alone was equipped with a thorough knowledge of the mysteries attendant to their upkeep.

Estrela moved through the interstices of the house as if guided by unseen hands. The confrontation with her father had been painless enough. She could only hope that he would fail to notice that the items on his desk were slightly out of order, that a crucial volume was missing from his library, that the insensible airs of his personal refuge had been inhabited by spirits unknown to him. She quietly recited her opening prayers as she made her way down a narrow passage. Her ardent desire for the emanations of the Holy One returned to her as she drew further from Esteban's presence. Soft waves of ivory fire spread throughout her body. The sensation originated in the space behind her breastbone and coursed through every limb and finger. The subtle force assuaged the swiftly fading remnants of her disappointment as if it were an anesthetic. She passed through a low doorway as her inner flame rose higher. It felt to her as if its increase would never end, neither subsiding nor diminishing until she was entirely consumed.

CPSIA information can be obtained
at www.ICGtesting.com
Printed in the USA
FFOW03n2353200518
46729447-48874FF